# BATTLE ON!

by Alan Arthur

Illustrations by Jason Berryman
(Pages 8, 15, 27, 31, 74, 92 and 114)

Cover photograph by L. M. Arthur

Published by
**Wilson Freelance**
1039 - 73 St.
Edmonton, Alberta
Canada
T6K 3M3



Printed in Canada
by Parkland ColorPress Ltd.

*Publisher's note: This work is a work of fiction, Although some actual place names do appear, and some characters may resemble actual people, the resemblances are purely coincidental, and there is no ill intent by the author, or the publisher.*

ISBN 0-9683020-0-9

*For*

Mom and Dad

# CONTENTS

# Introduction

Rivers and tales intertwine; rivers begetting tales, and tales glorifying rivers. The Mississippi, the Yangtze, the Amazon, the deified Ganges, and the Nile are but only a few of the planet's great tale rivers. Literally thousands of stories accompany each: religious, tall, fables, myths, adventures, lessons, and great literature. What would a Mark Twain yarn be without the Mississippi? Imagine Egypt without the Nile, or China without the Yangtze, or the famed Yellow. The river Thames, and the Blue Danube literally reek of a tale, just waiting to be told. Mystified, loved, beloved, glorified, glorious rivers, symbolizing the very essence of life itself.

"Bond. James Bond." In the background one can visualize, behind the Lotus, and the sexy damsel, if the fancying eye can get past Bond, or the damsel, the flowing smooth waters of an awesome river.

"I love you." is spoken only more, perhaps, in the light of the moon, or on a bed, than with a river behind.

Here, in this collection, we come upon the mighty Battle. Elegant intriguing name, conjuring up weapons, and wars, and indeed, the name itself, mighty battles. What an apt name for a river! Say it: "The Battle." No doubt many a vicious battle has occurred on the banks of a river such as the life-giving Nile, the mighty Amazon, or the wide Mississippi. No war history exists without the famed Bridge over a river. Movies are made, songs are sung, jokes are told. If a count of settings could be done in all of the literature of history, fact and fiction together, without a doubt, 'river' would be ranked highest, as ALL the important cities of the world are either on a major waterway, or where a waterway meets the sea. In theme, surely 'love' would take the award, unless of course death, or war, or sex.

But the Battle? Question someone. Ask them if they know of it.
"Not true. There is no such river."
"Remahkable name. Nevah erd of it." (James speaking.)
"Someone made it up. Pulling the leg, a little, are we?"

Only the locals know of it. And they don't care, much. For them, as with all locals, it is merely 'The River', as every cottage dweller has 'The Lake', and each mountain youth climbs 'The Mountain'.

Despite the grandiose silliness of the name, it indeed does exist, albeit a teeny thing in total contrast to its tag. A more suitable nomenclature would have been 'Tiny' or 'Long and Skinny', or 'Waterless' or 'Slow', or even a name of a discoverer, such as 'Williams' or 'Smith' or 'Windsor', or a Cree or Blackfoot name such as 'No-tin-to-si-ti', or 'Kinoka-kns-sis-ughty'. The poor thing, so small and helpless, shall never live up to itself. (In fact, history's best guess is that the name is derived from the English translation of Cree, Stoney, and Blackfoot words meaning 'where fighting takes place'. 'Battle' was first recorded on a map in 1803.) The Battle winds some 500 miles or so across the plains of Alberta, at the bottom of a glacial valley left behind at the last ice age. It's more of a mere creek, severely less than 'Battle' might suggest. This poor pathetic excuse of a river almost stops completely in dry years. It's not a river at all, some would say. If it weren't for the large drainage area, it probably would stop, a mere tinkle on the prairie, a raindrop in the dust, smaller yet than the pumpings from a well.

As a small child, for a few years, I did not realize that 'that' was the Battle, as we crossed it on the way to town, my imagination conjuring up something much more fantastic. When my mother came to understand my ignorance, and gently explained that 'that' indeed was the Battle, it was a major setback.

For the record, the old Battle begins as a trinkle overflow out of Battle Lake, and completes it's travels as a 10 metre across stream entering the North Saskatchewan at North Battleford, in Saskatchewan. It meanders slowly across north central Alberta, becoming Dried Meat Lake for a respite near the source, and then switching back and forth in endless curls at the bottom of it's valley, that bears the same moniker.

One not familiar with the works of glaciers would think that the tiny creek is totally unbefitting the valley, so much that in fact local folklore has as much to say about the Valley as the river itself. To the newcomer, the wuss of a river must be a major setback. It has a Tourist Zone named after it, stands out on all the maps and atlases, and even has had several books take its name, as if it were the Rocky Mountains, or the Grand Canyon, or some such marvel of nature. The poor goofy tourist, instead encounters this wee goof-off of a stream. Ha. Mama nature fooled Joe Tourist again. It's like calling a child playing construction site hillock a mountain, of some of those measly sloughs that urbanites like to name 'Lakes'.

"Those things aren't lakes. Lakes have other sides that you have to boat to; lakes you have to drive around. Lakes have fish in them. Urbanites, you silly twerps, why don't you put a sign up that tells the truth? Let the truth be told. Not 'Clearview Lake', but 'Clearview Dirty Pond', or 'Clearview Emergency Sewage Backup System', or 'Clearview Rainwater Reservoir'. Pathetic excuses for lakes. At least the Battle isn't man made, like those ghastly city sloughs.

# On Swimming

The Battle is a lazy river, and meanders back and forth across its own glacial valley. Each sharp corner has a hole, where the water is deeper, and can get to four metres or so. On straight stretches, often its bed is wide, and the water shallow, being as little as 8 inches at its deepest. In pioneer days, these spots became the fords for buggies, and wagons. The holes on the corners became swimming holes, and the deepest were avoided altogether. Sometimes current could play it's vicious taunting game of "Cross me if you can", and fast flowing spots were avoided as well, for fear of a young child being swept into water deeper than the neck. "People have drowned in it, you know," was the safety refrain from the elders. The oft repeated warning held truth, unfortunately, for the victims, and their loved ones. It's hard to swallow that such a creek could have taken anyone's life.

The ideal swimming hole, then, is one where the water is deep, but not too deep, where the current is minimal, and where there is a steep drop off, so that a diving board or platform can be constructed without the neck-breaking danger of diving into shallow water. These ideal spots only happen by nature once every few miles or so, and once they are found are held almost sacred by the locals, and given their own names, such as "The Hole", or "The Swimming Hole" if the locals aren't so creative. Better names are that of people or property owners like "Uncle Billy's Hole" or "King's Park". Sometimes a natural feature such as "The Snakebank", or up from the "Mouth of the Creek" fishing hole are used. Landmarks such as bridges or houses serve as reference points. My favorite names are attempts at humour such as "The Drowning Hole", or "The Naked Only Hole", or "Wreck Beach of the Battle". Other spots not so perilous are selected for families with small children, and because of the meandering nature of the river, most all chosen sites, perilous, and safe alike, are out of the way, known only to a few families, or friends, becoming almost private havens on public land.

Several parks, and campgrounds have been cleared and built along the old wanderer's banks, but most of these, built by man, are logically close to highways, for access, not because of the natural swimming holes. Nope, not too many great swimming hangouts there. Besides, who would dare skinny dip at a public beach?

For a few select souls, mostly young men who live or lived close enough to the river to be able to venture down without a driver's license, because of the distance to the nearest constabulary, swimming becomes a ritualistic event of every evening throughout the months of July and August, when school and its conventions lose their grip over collective consciousness, and the freedom of the prairie river holds sway in school's stead.

# On Fishing

The first time I heard that joke, it was told to me, appropriately, by none other than a one armed fisherman. He *knew* that he could get away with whatever political incorrectness it might bring. But it never fails to get a chuckle, or an "Aw, sick," reaction. It does prove that fishing is somewhat of a universal activity for all kinds of people the world over, whether for survival, or for relaxation. To this day, I do not know whether my one armed friend had actually been fishing, or was just using his disability to humour the rest of us. I assumed, at the time, that he had been fishing. However, those were naive days, and in retrospect the old geezer may have pulled one over on a young fellow.

Another short fishing anecdote I can relate comes from the Indian Ocean isle of Mauritius, where amongst the locals, fish are thought to have spirits guiding them, so each sincere fisherman makes an offering to the fish spirits before he goes out, in this case, to the ocean, for the day. Usually the offering is a cigarette, and the fisherman puts it at the base of a seaside tree, such as a palm, where the spirit dwells for the evening. One person who I associated with there, when we were discussing the ritual, queried, "If the fisherman leaves a cigar, will he not catch a bigger fish?"

Fishing in the Battle River is a cyclic thing. Populations and species vary every few years. Sucker, goldeye, walleye, some minnow species, and the famed slough shark (pike) all seem to take their turns, and populations ebb and flow. There is some debate whether they come upstream from the North Saskatchewan by way of North Battleford, downstream from Dried Meat Lake south of Camrose, or actually winter in some of the deeper holes. Locals suspect all three may be true to some extent. If one wishes, he could speak to a government game biologist, who would be sure to give you all the facts, as these guys know everything, being from the big city and all. For example they know that blue herrings are solitary birds, and never nest in groups, always in tops of trees, and that bear, moose, and elk NEVER wander into this river valley.

"If you do hear of it, the locals are pulling your leg. Guys know nothing."

"That moose you saw wasn't a moose."

"Guy must have got that picture from somewhere else."

The point is you should trust the experts, if they so define themselves that way. Just like you should trust politicians.

Whatever the claims may be by expert or local alike, the fish *are* there, as most anyone who has ever tried his luck once or twice over any time span at all, will attest. One ol' fisherman who fished during the late 60s claimed to have once caught 73 (53 walleye, and 20 pike, so he said) on a single Sunday afternoon, with the help of a few walleye eyes for bait, and kid fishermen wannabes.

The fish are not recommended for eating, as the river is part of the North Saskatchewan system, and it is now polluted, sadly, perhaps beyond repair. Two or three wouldn't hurt. They look healthy enough, except for that greenish puss stuff hanging out of ol' slough shark's jaw, and the stream itself appears healthy, at least on years there is continuous water flow, if it weren't for the algae. Algae increases with dryness and drought. But who knows how much mercury and dioxins lie beneath the pike's gills. Only die hard survivalists eat slough shark, anyway. The species goldeye, according to the pollution watchers, retains more mercury than do other species. In keeping with recreational ecology, today most fish from or of the Battle are thrown back in, to live another year, or at least until the next hole, and next line.

The fishing is best in spring and in fall. The summer is too hot and sluggish. In the spring, once all the mud clears up, the pike get active, favoring any place they can see further than a couple of inches in front of their eyes, such as the mouths of creeks or springs. Stupid things will even eat others of the same species that are larger than themselves. That's the truth. One can see an Escher geometric drawing based on three ravenous pike, each with a tail of one of his own, in his gaping jaws. Only creature on earth besides a real shark that has a larger mouth than the his own circumference anywhere else on his body. Except for that snake that eats those huge eggs.

In the fall, most species gather in eddy holes after rapids, catching anything drifting past, or on corners on the outside of the curve, where the force of the water makes it deeper. Slough sharks like underwater trees, and hiding spots.

Walleye, and goldeye prefer the rapids, over gravelly rocks, and love to lie low near the bottom. Wally and Goldy are a bit trickier to catch as they won't eat just anything, unlike their stupid bigmouthed cousin the slough shark, who will eat fingers while on people, women's jewelry, baby ducks, eggs, baseballs, caps, berries, or rocks tossed in, and can be caught on any device at all, provided it has the two key ingredients: movement, and a hook.

More than one fisherman has disdainfully claimed, "The largest walleye I ever did catch was in the belly of a darned pike."

The sucker is not a gamefish as a rule, as it won't bite a lot, but still the poor sucker fishermen try and catch it, by snagging, or by illegal netting on creeks or the river itself. They have been seen from shore in large schools of 50 odd, and are generally considered even dumber than ol' slough shark himself.

I have seen no recorded evidence of any other species such as sturgeon, trout, perch, or bass, but it wouldn't be terribly surprising if someone, somewhere, claimed their existence, by telling a story.

* * * *

## On Characters

"He was a character all right."

If someone, in reflective reminiscing, says that, the listener knows the person to whom was just referred must have been something special. Ordinary people are not characters. Only those with unique attributes, usually more than one unique attribute, are called that. The usual stereotype for the statement involves an elderly experienced man, often a bachelor, but not necessarily, and often outspoken, or at least having a memorable aura about them. A non-conformist, in some way.

The Battle Valley has had, (and continues to have, I suppose) its share of them. For it was at one time, a place away from civilization, where uniqueness is allowed to flourish, where the 'civilized' society's expectations are rare, if not downright nonexistent. In pioneer days, much time was spent alone or within the family group, away from the others, hence there was little pressure to conform, or need to conform, a self reliant existence being all that one needed for survival. If a person had one particular skill, and was skilled at it, that was sufficient. Today, survival usually dictates being more well rounded

To not follow the rules was not encouraged, but it more or less just happened, because of the lack of socialization, and in some cases, lack of law enforcement. Prairie society, as a whole perhaps was richer because of this. Most certainly these souls added diversity to the spectrum of man. They covered all facets of personality: evertalking braggarts, silent hermits, freeloading wanderers, filthy beggars, marvelous storytellers, unscrupulous crooks, illegal moonshiners, hound owners, and horse trainers, to categorize but a few. This menagerie just scratches the surface.

Ah, but regardless of the poor victim river not holding up to its title (Battle) or definition of geographic feature (River) does not mean it does not or should not have tales of its own. Tales, after all are borne of people, not geographic features. Where there are people, there are tales. Tales are weird things, you know. They can be as true as curves on a woman, or they can be as false as curves on a woman. Either way, they are meant to entertain, to educate, to unravel mysteries, or simply to kill the passing hours, keeping others entertained. The answer to the age old question of truthhood or falsehood lies only in the taleteller. Even that may be distorted or questioned over time, as what the teller believes he saw and actually saw may indeed change with age, or with the number of times the tale is told. To determine truth in a tale is part of the joy.

As Great Uncle Harold always began his oral tradition tales with the same line, "Now this is the absolute truth," so too did we kids smile at the knowledge that of what was about to enter our naive ears would indeed be entertaining, if not the whole truth, or even anything close.

This particular tale collection takes it's origin from somewhere near the town of Wainwright, or Hardisty, or Camrose, or Galahad. This information regarding origin, however, does not imply that these stories would be or are unique to the measly Battle River, for river tales are universal in their appeal. Change the name of the river, and of the towns, of the country, if you wish. It matters not.

# Clam Bake

Visions of clam bakes danced in their heads. So what if no one understood the real clam bake, like on Prince Edward Island. They'd all heard of it, being Canadian and all. Literature was full of references to Maritimers having a party on the beach, baking clams, and revelling. "Can't be that hard." said Lou's Papa. "Bake a clam. Big deal."

The suggestion had arisen moments earlier from his daughter, Lou, who was here for her first time, and had just discovered that this river held clams, and lots of them. A mental imagery connection to the Maritime clam bake had manifested inside her dreamy head, leading her to pursue it with the wondrous sounding words, "Let's have a clam bake." Following the apex of creation were numerous shouts of agreement from cousins, brothers, and sisters all. "Yes, let's!" said one cousin.

"What a great idea!" said another.

In the muddy banks and bottom of the Battle exists the prehistoric creature, the river clam, some distant relative to the Maritime clam, but a clam all the same. Remnants of the simple beast, in the form of shiny shells can be found all along the river. To find living ones is trickier. When the water is clear at midsummer, they leave tracks in the sandy bed, and you can follow the track, until finding the clam. That takes awhile, perhaps two or three hours to get but a few. Better yet to go to the river's deepest spot, and dive. Hidden in the bottom mud amidst the rocks they dwell, although unable to do much, except hide in the bottom. Either that or go to a muddy bank just off shore, and below the surface a foot or so, dig in the mud, and lo, there's clams. They make excellent playmates for the bored lolling swimmer, and have many uses, none of which are functional, other than recreation. You can have clam skipping contests, or clam castle building contests, races to find who can collect the most in an alloted time, or find partially open ones to squeeze out water, pretending the clam is urinating. No wonder clams became the money of ancient peoples.

If clams were currency today, then the kids at this clam bake would be rich, as there is nothing quite so abundant, in the right place, of course, as the dull ol' Battle River clam. Within fifteen minutes, they had collected from the depths and banks, some 100, probably more, of the would be delectables up on shore near the fire.

"Finally, we have a purpose for these things," commented Deryl, Lou's cousin and self appointed president of the clam picker's union. "If this turns out, Uncle Bob, you have to pay us for them, and pay us when we start selling, and marketing them."

"Tell you what, young fellow. Your pay today will be a fine meal of free clams." responded Uncle. "After that, we'll see."

Once the horde of saucer shapes was stacked neatly beside the fire, in castle shape, Lou put forth the inevitable, "Does anyone here actually know how to do a clam bake?"

Papa knew just what to say. He'd heard. Never been there, actually, but grapevine knowledge is as good as it gets, in these circumstances, anyway. No one else seemed to be coming forth with reams of encyclopedic or experential knowledge."

"First you have to dig a big pit in the sand." Giving directions was his forte, especially to kids who followed, wide-eyed, and willing.

"What for, Uncle Bob?" asked the union president.

"You have to bury the clams in the sand beneath hot coals." Geez, Uncle Bob knew everything.

"Well, what are we waiting for?" Deryl looked at the crew of cousins who had gathered around, each having made his or her own contribution to the pile. "Let's dig the hole."

He selected a spot within clam chucking distance, marked out a yard wide circle with his toe, and bossed, "Dig it right here. Then he turned back to the expert, and asked, "How deep do we need it, Uncle?"

"Usually about three feet or so, but with this many clams, maybe a bit more. You'll need lots of room for all those clams."

"Okay," came the chorus. They began the labor immediately, all six of them, in a circle, digging with hands only, using fingernails to labor away, like only gophers can, bums up in six directions. This kind of co-operation yields the most admirable of results, and in this case it was a hole, deep and wide, enough to hold a thousand clams. Twenty minutes later they all stood proudly around the great clam bake hole.

"Now what?" asked the foreman.

"Now we need to get a bunch of hot coals into the bottom of the pit, so the clams can be cooked from the bottom up." The expert was getting more expert like, explaining it more to them.

"We need the fire bigger, guys. We'll need a whole bunch more wood. Let's go over to that bush, and get as many dead trees as we can." Off they hurried, together co-operating to take down four or five inch trees which were no longer connected well to roots, and in pairs of manly laborers, hauling them back to the fire, which soon became so roaring that the expert, and his adult companions, moved further back. No one complained of the scratches on backsides or bellies, for all this work would surely whet an appetite, and the clams would be go down smoother.

Once the roaring fire had burned down so one could see the hot coals, the foreman asked, "How can we get the coals into the pit, Uncle?"

Not forgetting any details, the expert told him, "You run up to my half ton on the hill there, and there's a spade in the back. You, but only you, because you're the only one strong enough, can shovel a bunch of the coals into the pit."

Realizing his work crew was tired from the brush removal, the foreman showed his true leadership skills, and hustled right on over to the Chevy to do as he was told, brought back the spade, and proceeded to start moving the hot coals across the sand, by sliding the spade under them, and dragging the coals along the sand until they toppled into the pit. After he thought he had sufficient coals, he asked, "How many coals do we need in here, Uncle?"

"Probably you need a few more than that. The fires will go out, and the clams will need to bake about two hours. Put just a few more in." Uncle directed. Deryl obeyed. Then he gathered his crew, now refreshed from their break, and ordered them to move the clams in, while he took a Kool-Aid break, which they eagerly did, by tossing the saucer like objects into the target, a smoldering pit of hot embers. Progress was being made for the feast.

"Now what?" asked Deryl, of the experet, when this, probably the easiest, and certainly the most enjoyable part was done.

"Throw in a more coals. We want it to get really hot down there, don't we?"

Deryl wondered why Uncle wasn't helping much. "You know, Uncle Bob, you haven't done much work. I don't know if you deserve to eat a clam when all this is done. The rest of us have done all the work." He started moving more hot coals, and half burning logs, by now having shovel blisters on his hands.

"But I've been the co-ordinator. Without my advice, none of this could have happened," Uncle Bob reminded him. "Besides, whose spade is that?"

"Yeah, I guess you're right. Besides, I figure there will be plenty of clams to go around. There are ten people here, and that's about ten clams each." He had mentally calculated each person's share, including all the other adults, who hadn't even bothered to lift a finger.

"Now you have to cover the whole thing up, so that all the heat will stay down there, and they'll bake." Uncle Bob's contributions were essential.

"How? If we just throw a bunch of sand in, won't the clams get all sandy? We don't want to get a bunch of sand in the clams, do we?" Deryl needed more advice.

The instructor provided it. "Oh, no, silly boy. First you have to go collect a bunch of greenery, mostly green leaves. They will make a barrier between the sand and the clams. Also, they'll provide moisture and steam so the clams will cook properly."

Once again, the foreman gathered his crew, and went for green leaves. They found willow, which had ideal bendable branches to form a criss cross pattern, and Russian poplar, which had larger leaves, which could be laid out on the willow, to make an impenetrable barrier from the sand to come. He instructed two girls to lay in the willow, first a bunch parallel, and then another layer perpendicular, like a lattice fence. The girls found this work enjoyable, because it was artsy craftsy, even though it was hot close to the pit. As they added more willow, the heat began to dry it out, and smoke started billowing from the pit.

On a leaf carrying trip back to the pit, Deryl realized this was causing a problem. "Come on, you guys, hurry up. We have to get all the leaves in before the willow all burns up!"

After two more trips to the bushes to get leaves, all six of the clam bakers helped to push in the leaves, across the sand, making the barrier. Clouds of smelly smoke from the drying Russian poplar leaves billowed from the circle, which had now become much larger than Deryl had originally drawn on the sand, due to cave-ins from the edges from the trampling about.

Deryl proceeded to shovel in sand now, from the piles from the original pit, which was simple because the sand was loose, and close at hand, although some had been packed down from all the foot traffic about.

"Wow, that's it!" he exclaimed after the last shovel covered the final remaining wisp of smoke. He moved over to the main fire picnic area to rest and admire. "Now I guess all we have to do is wait, eh, Uncle?"

"That's right. In two hours or so, you guys can dig it all up, and there will be clams to feast on." Uncle appeared to be looking forward to this as much as Deryl.

The two hours could not go fast enough. Before the first hour was up, the youngest member of the overworked crew returned to ask Uncle Bob, who was doing timing duty, "How much more time before they're ready?"

Uncle Bob glanced at his wrist. "At least another hour, Bill. You might as well go back swimming for a while. I'll call everybody when the time is up."

Uncle Bob didn't need to call anyone. At twenty minutes before the appointed time, all the group had gathered around eagerly anticipating the great feast.

Finally, with the precision timing of an explosive device, Uncle Bob announced, "Time's up. They're ready." No one noticed his lack of a timing device.

Back on their hands and knees, the youngsters gathered around to paw, as they had originally. Only this time they encountered some dead wood, steam, and hot sand. Lou gave up first, "Everything's too hot, Deryl. You'll have to dig them up with the shovel."

"Okay," Deryl agreed, and retrieved the shovel, but his first attempts to get to the now cooked succulent morsels were blocked by semi-dried sticks of green willow. Lou and her artsy colleague, who had together constructed the lattice, reached in from the edges of the pit, and grabbed ends of sticks, which were still green, and tossed them haphazardly away in the opposite direction from where the peering others gathered to view the pile of cooked goodies.

Soon the shovel made a clunking sound, as if hitting a stone. It was the clams. Deryl pushed hard on the shovel, at the close side of the pit, and retrieved a sordid mixture that included green and dry leaves, lots of sand, a partially burned root, and two treasured delights, the goal of the whole affair. He dumped the mess out of the shovel.

Lou went over, and picked up one of the clams for closer inspection. Its shell was partially opened from the heat, but she could not open the rest of it. "How do you get it open, Dad?" she asked the expert.

"I guess you have to pull really hard, Dear. Let someone stronger try."

She gave the thing to Deryl, who also couldn't manage to open it. He could peer through the crack between shells to see the soft part, the part to eat. This was frustrating. The clam was behind a fortified wall of shell, yet it was right there, so close, yet uncatchable. "Do you have any more tools in your truck we can use, Uncle?" Surely the fellow who had managed to escort them this far would be able to solve one more minor problem.

"You can go up, and take a look, if you like." Uncle was always generous with tools. Whatever he had could be shared by family members. Deryl appreciated that about his Uncle.

"Thanks, Uncle Bob," he yelled, as be ran off to obtain some necessary more items. In the meantime, Uncle, to show that he wasn't so lazy, got up, and proceeded to dig out several more treasures from the pit. All of the treasures appeared in about the same condition as the first. Some were more charred, and some were cracked further open. Before Deryl returned, Lou even found one that split wide. She separated it completely, using one side as a saucer to hold the soft tissue about for all to admire.

"Gross," remarked little Bill, and he spoke for everyone. The clam appeared either uncooked, or overcooked, and not at all appetizing.

"I think we should wait for Deryl. He's done most of the work. He should get the thrill of eating the first clam," she so thoughtfully announced, even though since the whole thing had been her idea, she probably had the right of first try. The announcement came as relief for the others, who collectively sighed.

Deryl made his way down the hill, arms loaded with a crowbar, a pitchfork, a hammer, and a foot long chisel. The latter two tools he had found inside Uncle's tool box in the truck. The tool box was normally out of bounds to the kids, but in this special circumstance, he felt Uncle wouldn't mind. "These things ought to help," he announced upon arrival at the scene.

Lou had to break the news. "While you were gone, we actually got one open, Deryl."

He was only a tad disappointed. "Really? Who ate the first one?"

Lou apologized. "We kept it for you because you should have the first one." She held it out to him.

"Well, that was mighty nice of you," he thanked, and took it from her, she being eager to give the wretched thing away.

He held the shell in his left hand, and lifted it to his nose. "Smells pretty fishy like," he said, "hope they aren't poisonous." A crowd had gathered to stare at the human guinea pig performing his best dramatic rite. Initiation into the world of clam. There are those that have, and those that haven't. He was about to cross to the other side of lore, and was brilliant in the attainment of witnesses to the feat. To think a Maritime custom could happen here on the shores of his tiny river. Such drama! A veritable last spike.

He found a clumpy part, away from guts, and head, and poked it into his mouth with his right hand, which had to be agile in it's grip, as the clam was slippery, as in a bowl of oiled jelly. He managed to get a portion inside his waiting mouth, without the entire parcel falling to the sand below, which would have ruined the whole event. Imagining it to be soft, like chicken, he bit with little force, at first. Each time he bit, the teeth would bounce back to their original position. After three attempts to bite through, he pulled it back out, commenting, "This thing is pretty tough, sort of rubbery."

"What does it taste like?" asked Lou.

"I can't really tell," Deryl responded. "I haven't really gotten any into my mouth yet."

"Try the gooey part, then," suggested cousin Lou, who wanted only vicarious experience, inwardly glad it was he, not her, but outwardly appearing to be right next in line.

"Well, there's a lot of sand in that part. I don't know if I can get straight juice," he observed.

"But you have to try, or we won't even know what it tastes like," she encouraged.

He used his tongue to lick some of the juice out of the natural bowl, getting only a few grains of sand on the tip. "Ooh. Tastes pretty weird." The unfamiliar half rotten fleshy taste caused his face to distort in the manner of disgust. But his oral language, caused by adolescent hero nature, forced it different, "Not bad, actually." Then he spit it out, without swallowing.

"What exactly does it taste like?" Lou didn't really want to know, but felt obliged to ask, even if his face had already answered the question.

"Uh," he paused, not being able to find a comparable subconscious memory to suit, "I guess it tastes a bit like clam." At this he smiled at his own play stupid joke.

"Well, I guess it should," agreed Sue.

Now that the juice was gone, he tried again to bite it through, but to no avail. The thing was tougher than a rubber hose, like a pile of silicon caulking gone all rubbery hard. Inedible. Completely, for reason of toughness. Might just as well swallow a rubber ball. At least it would probably pass through without any internal damage to intestines. The clam may have gotten lodged somewhere.

Eventually, two others, boy cousins, in boy heroism, but unable to repeat the drama of Deryl, followed his lead, and tasted the juice, but were unable to bite through the muscle part. They suffered similarly, which brought childhood bonding to the three.

When the time came to leave the Maritime richness behind, and return home to boring prairie life, Deryl remembered to appreciate his uncle's helpful hints. "Thanks, Uncle Bob, for letting us use all your stuff. We couldn't have done it without you."

"No problem, son, no problem at all," replied Uncle Bob, with that quirky grin.

# The Engineer

Peter was destined to be an engineer, to design bridges, buildings, and towers. Summers of his childhood on the farm were spent building: rafts on barrels, underground forts, and three tiered treehouses. In winter, the summer projects were replaced by hockey rinks, straw bale castles, and snow igloos. The availability of tools like axes, hammers, spikes, and shovels allowed his creative energy to manifest in one structure or another, depending on his personal whim of the day, or week. Some structures remained unfinished, others were altered and re-altered from one summer to the next. Most disappeared when the materials found a new use, or another project was more interesting. Remnants of his original designs remained on the farm long after he became a real engineer.

Summer evenings, once he learned how to drive, were spent with friends down at the Battle, where a few years earlier a 'perfect' swimming hole had been hit upon, and held in memory, for the time he could drive down himself. The perfect hole was isolated from the world, along an old trail some five miles from a main road. It took another quarter of a mile of bush to walk to, but was worth the scratches from bush. The river was wide, and slow, below a rapid, but for some reason about five feet deep, and flat all the way across, except for, of course, near each bank, where the depths increased rapidly, but not as much as at a banked curve. The hole was superb for water football, or water polo.

One Sunday afternoon, when Peter and three friends were taking a break on the beach from the roughhousing football game, one of them, Kenny, in a relaxed mood simply said, "What this place needs is a diving board."

To Peter this was divine inspiration. In a spot where the water got deeper faster, a diving board would be easier, as you just had to extend a plank, out from the bank. Here, he would need to build the whole structure out into the water, which created more engineering problems. Just the kind of thing engineers do!

The usual games were getting boring, and this was after all, his very own forte. For exactly a week, his mind hashed over various structures, and many possibilities. He was the head engineer, the boss, and he had to factor in several problems: current, sandy bottom, water depth, tool limitations, labor, and the design itself.

The current was slow here so he figured it wouldn't be a difficult thing to overcome. He had his strong friends to help. The sandy bottom would continue to cave in if they tried to dig, but he figured they could work fast enough to pound in two posts about five feet out from the shore, that would be stable enough for this purpose. For tools, he could borrow everything he needed from Dad: hammers, the post pounder, the axe, the bucksaw, spikes, shovels, and rope. They would cut straight poplars for the scaffolding. The one thing that he might have to harangue from Dad would be a plank, just for the top, so that the divers would have a stable platform to jump or dive from.

"Dad, do you think we could take one of those leftover planks from the pile by the shed? We want to build a diving platform by the river."

"Sure, Peter, just bring it back when you're finished with it at the end of summer." Dad could see in Peter's eyes that another one of 'those projects' was being constructed in that everworking mind.

Over the week he gathered the materials, going over and over the intricacies of construction. Sunday finally came, and the four of them headed out.

"Peter, what's all that stuff for?" Ken inquired.

"Don't you remember? Last Sunday you said that our hole needed a diving board. Well, we're building it this week."

"Okay." Kenny sounded skeptical, but what the heck, he knew Peter well enough to know that this might just work. He'd seen some other creations like the three tiered treehouse with the liftable ladder to ward off invader girls, or the two pitted fort that had two holes in the ground, one covered with a board roof, and a tunnel between the two, about ten feet down. The friend became a willing volunteer.

At the river, the crew toiled away, with foreman Peter barking out instructions. The first task was to find four straight poplar trees, each about 12 feet long, to serve as corner posts for the structure. Two would be sunk into the ground on the shore, and two more would have to be sunk out in the water. The plan was to get these four posts in first, and then brace, brace, and brace, like scaffolding, building up from the ground, all the while maintaining stability.

After four suitable trees were chopped, sharpened, and drug out of the bushes, some measurements were taken, and a few more smaller trees chopped, which would serve as bracing, both between the two sets of poles, and as angular bracing. Better solid than shaky. Peter didn't need anyone on the construction site getting injured, or worse, have the whole thing collapse while someone was climbing to the top, or diving. Lots of these poles had sharp ends.

The first two poles in the ground on shore were easy. All you had to do was dig into the soft sand until you hit the water level, then twist the poles to work them in deeper, and hence solidify them. Once these two were in place, the next task was to get the two out in the water in. For this, he had to use more ingenuity. Two of the stronger fellows held the post at the bottom, all the while twisting it into the sand below a foot or so of water, and fighting the current, while a third held on to a rope attached to the top of the pole, from on shore upstream, where he could have better traction, and help fight the current. Peter, by himself would manage to hold up the bracing smaller pole, and spike it together. First one and then the other. In the beginning the whole thing was unstable, but with sufficient crossbracing between all four corners, and corner-bracing in all directions, eventually the complete structure unfolded. It had two levels of bracing, one about four feet from the ground, and then the top level, some eight feet above ground. Construction lasted the whole afternoon, but when it was completed, the four members of the crew took a moment to stand back and admire their work.

"Well, there's our diving platform. What do you think?" Peter was as proud as Buckminster Fuller.

"It's great," marvelled Kenny.

"I'd say it's a masterpiece of building," added Jerome.

"The best thing is we have it to use all summer now. We can get some inner tubes to dive through. This takes the cake." added Nick.

"So Peter has to have the first dive. He's the boss." Kenny informed the others.

Peter proudly scaled the back part, commenting on the way up, ever the improver, "We need to build a ladder thing back here," and stood on top, arms up in victory gesture. The contraption was a tad shaky, but as long as it wasn't going to break or tumble, it would do just fine. With a mighty "YAHOO!" he jumped as far out into the stream as he could, not wanting to dive just yet, until he tested the depth safety of the water upon impact from so far up. The crowd cheered.

For the rest of the afternoon, all half hour of it, the boys reveled in their own ingenuity, and took turns diving, jumping, cannonballing, twisting, and trying flips. Scores were given in a jumping creativity contest, and they held a 'how far out you can leap' competition, arguing in pal ways over how to make a fair mark in the water. The afternoon had to end all too soon. Fortunately, there were evenings, and next Sunday. Next time the platform would be ready upon arrival. There would be no more building to do, except for Peter's ladder at the back, which really wasn't necessary.

Farm work didn't allow for the friends to meet again until the following Sunday. Peter drove the truck almost too fast on the way down. Together they rushed to the site, inner tubes readied for the fresh afternoon of diving.

Upon coming into view of the previous week's work, they stopped short. The masterpiece was still there, only today it had a dreadful forward lean to it. The front part had seemingly been lowered a foot or two, and the plank was still on top, but only because Peter had hammered a couple of nails into it. Fortunately. Otherwise the plank would have slid right into the river.

"What happened?" asked Kenny.

"Well, it's busted, that's for sure." Peter's eyes showed a mixture of sadness, yet pride. Even looking like the leaning diving tower of Piza, it still held some magnificence, as per the week before.

"Maybe the current made the front poles dig deeper into the sand, kinda like quicksand," suggested Kenny.

Peter got closer. "Nope, that's not it. Look at this." He pointed to the bottoms of the two front poles. Teeth marks. Beaver teeth marks. Some wise beaver buddy had taken advantage of the situation, having not to even climb out of the water to get a fresh bark feast, and a couple of poles.

"All that work for nothing," lamented Jerome.

For the next moments, more unfavorable adjectives than for rats were placed in front of the noun beaver, many of them unprintable.

"And we don't have any tools to fix it." Peter was ever the Mr. Fix-it.

"I wonder what the stupid beaver thought when the tree didn't fall on him." Kenny pondered.

In time, with Peter's wit, and determination to not give in to the rodent, Mr. Beaver's personality transformed into an almost respectable one, given his opportunistic ways. After all, he was only a beaver. Peter expressed his halfway admiration, "Well, think about it. If you were a beaver, and you were swimming along here, and saw these handy dandy two trees, just sticking out of the water, wouldn't you have done the same thing? It's not really the beaver's fault."

"Oh, don't be so kind. Stupid beaver oughta be shot. Too bad the plank didn't fall and konk him on his measly hairy head." Kenny wasn't so admiring.

"We should find his house, and set a trap by it. That would stop him from doing it again."

"There's probably more than one anyway. Who knows where their house might be? It could be a half mile or more from here. There are lots of beavers on this river." Peter was more logical. "Besides, it's my fault."

"How is it your fault? You didn't wreck it." Kenny blamed beavers.

"I didn't plan for it. That's why it's my fault. I planned for everything else, like the current, and all that. I plum forgot about beavers. That's all."

"So what's the plan now, big fellow?" Kenny wanted to see some humor in all this work for nothing."

"Oh, don't worry. I have a plan." Peter did.

"And is it going to involve about four more hours of our manpower?" Kenny wasn't so eager to participate this time around. "The last plan kind of collapsed."

"Well, next week we'll just put it up again, just the two poles in the water. In fact I think we can just use the existing structure. Dad has some old stovepipe. I'll just pound the pipe around the posts to about a foot above water level. We'll see if those beavers can gnaw their way through metal."

It took another week for the revised plan to manifest, but Peter proved to be correct. "That'll show them!" he stated emphatically when the job was done.

Sure enough, the week after that, the structure was still standing erect, the rebuilt non-leaning water tower of Piza. The tin around the bottom was intact, except for a couple of beaver size tooth mark dents in the tin.

# Corn Man

Not all years are splendid growing years in east central Alberta, due to drought, and the length of the growing season. In the south, around Taber, drought is overcome by irrigation, and the growing season is longer naturally, so 95% of the time, perhaps more, the garden vegetables such as corn, the eating from the cob variety, not the cowfeed, or popcorn varieties of the Yanks, can be produced in ways unequaled on the planet. Not so here. An early frost, or a late spring can undo dreams, and drought can make the dreams one third the size of normal. The villains of Mother nature, together, could, and have made many a farm gardener come to tears from their collective wickedness.

However, on the good years....now that's when Mother Nature's angels, the Sun, and moisture, get together in the spirit of co-operation, and leave gardeners prouder than skunks squirting hounds, with abundant hordes of earthy green, orange, and red marvels, of domesticated plants, true homage examples of what She can do, with their lustrous aid.

The Williams sisters, Ellen and May, had kept their families close for years. Each had married men of the area, and had settled into the agriculture mixed farming lifestyle, each bearing five children, and working arduous 17 hour days on the two farms, tending to the milking, the gardens, and the mischievous children, whilst the men did their own hard work in the fields, trying just to make a go of it. The brothers-in-law co-operated with machinery, and labor intensive projects such as haying. Sundays were often days off, and the whole group, all fourteen of them, would meet at either home, or sometimes, in summer, on the shores of the Battle.

One particular Sunday such was the case. An urbanite from Regina, Ellen's brother-in-law, Roy, and his family of five, including himself, and his wife, were holidaying for a few days, giving 'these city kids' a chance to explore farm life. More cousins to find trouble with. More mouths to feed. More heads to count. Regina, although western enough, was still urban, and at that time fresh veggies, although available, never approached the quality of the two hour old home grown delectable, so Ellen planned a veritable feast, and she coerced her sister May to join them, hence making for a sizeable family gathering on the Battle. The sisters got together midweek, and knowing the work involved, decided to keep things simple, yet bountiful in quantities. "I'll bring hamburger, and buns, if you can just bring fresh corn and potatoes. That way we can feed everyone to their belly's content, but still have time for visiting."

May agreed wholeheartedly, as simplicity was the key to saving time, and this was not a time for work. The men could do most of the heavy work out there, anyway, with their egos re firebuilding, and barbecuing.

From fishing the river, Ellen's husband Will knew of a special place that had enough flat area to allow for lots of fire room, had shallow safe water for the young 'uns to mess about in, and was an easy walk through the bushes, which contained lots of deadfall for the fires.

About two in the afternoon, two mixed up carloads of cousins pulled into May's place, and within three or four minutes, three carloads of further mixed up cousins left in the direction of the river. "Make up your damn minds where you want to ride!" Roy had yelled at the milling about pack, mostly in jest anger, but they didn't know that, so each had piled into the back of whichever vehicle was closest, meaning one carload had six in the back, and another only had two. It mattered not, just so long as the trunks were loaded down with food, and the insatiable appetites of the whole horde could be satisfied.

Not to worry. The sisters had counted heads earlier, "six adults, thirteen children," and had thrown in enough farm fare to supply two heavy hamburgers, five fresh young tasty potatoes, and three delicious cobs of corn per person, just in case. To overdo it was the custom. Besides, one could always take it home for tomorrow. Just so long as the rear shocks under the trunk held. The appetites would be out in full force, they knew, because water, and water activity, just does that to healthy young bodies, for some odd reason.

The weather was perfect, about 80 degrees, when they arrived. All the kids piled out, and headed for the river, but Roy stopped them all with a mighty bellow, "What the heck do you think you're all doing? How do you know that water's safe?"

"Damn that uncle from the city," they thought, but stopped anyway, out of respect, or fear, maybe both.

"You need an adult like me to inspect it first. See if it doesn't have any holes, or too much current. We sure as heck don't need any drownings." His powerful voice had let up a bit, now that he had their attention. "I want you kids to all stay on the shore here until I check it out. I can swim, learned it in the army, as far as I know, none of you kids can, at least not very well."

One of his nieces was growing impatient, having tolerated several 'army' lectures all week long, "Well, then Uncle Roy, get on with it. Check it out." she said, somewhat with hesitation. Her siblings admired her courage, but were grateful for her, the youngest, who always seemed able to charm him with her questions.

"Well, that's just what I'm gonna do, Honey," he replied, as he waded in. "You guys all stay here until I get across, and then I'll wave to tell you if it's safe or not." The opposite bank was only some thirty yards away, within easy shouting distance, but what the heck, if he wants to do this, we'll let him, they all thought. No point arguing or we might all be headed for home or banned from swimming, put in military jail, here on the Battle's banks.

Two of the older boycousins looked at each other, and rolled their eyes. "Was he a sargeant?" one of May's kids, who didn't know him as well, whispered.

"Yes," nodded the week long recruit, now experienced, at least for a week longer than his inquisitive cousin.

Roy kept wading, the water not yet up to his knees, and was midstream before he yelled back, "It's okay so far, guys!" in another thirty seconds, he reached the other side, and the knees still weren't wet.

The leadership bravado fell short of any real heroism, but he maintained his dignity and managed to yell back, once his feet touched the grass on the far shore, "It's totally safe for you kids. Just don't go upstream or downstream very far," he cautioned, still.

With the clearance for takeoff, all thirteen ready and waiting youngsters rushed their eager, and sun dried bodies in, and began splashing each other about in childhood play, the courageous versus the meek. Roy, too, came back, to join in the fun, hunting down the few still dry female victims, and making sure they all received ample water to dirty their hair.

Meanwhile, back on the beach, the other five adults, having momentarily enjoyed Roy's misguided attempt at leadership of his newly found soldiers in Battle, began to prepare for the feast, by making two rock circles for two separate fires.

"Go bring us all the stuff from all the trunks," commanded Ellen, of Will, and her brother-in-law on her side.

"After that, you can build us a couple of huge fires in these pits," added May. Realizing that the women probably needed the break more than they did, and would surely be doing more than their share of cooking within the hour, the two men did as they were commanded. Ellen and May had better soldiers than Roy did, at least ones that obeyed, and followed out commands.

Soon the two men had the cookery assembled, and decided to head for the cool water as well, to cool off, and enjoy the play.

"Might as well cook that corn first, Ellen," suggested May, and I'll start making hamburger patties out of all this meat. Then if those critters (kids) come in for a snack before it's ready, they can have a cob of that to hold them until later."

The first guest to arrive back on shore was Roy. "Those kids don't need me out there any more, they're fine," he announced to the women, as he came ashore.

May smiled at her sister to indicate, "Yeah, right. He needed them more than they needed him. It's okay, though. We're having fun."

"Anything to eat yet?" he asked, as the frolic had whetted his appetite.

"Not really, except some corn. You want one?" answered May.

"Sure," he smiled.

She dabbed one of the steaming cobs out with a prong, handed it to him, saying, "I think Ellen has some butter over there on the table," and gestured to Ellen's table.

"Hunt in the box, and you'll find it," commanded Ellen.

He did as he was told, and finding salt as well, smeared a bunch on the cob, and bit in. "Wow, this is excellent corn, May," he complimented, between mouthfuls. Salty saliva, mixed with minuscule bits of chewed corn, trinkled from the corners of his mouth, only to be recaptured by a burly curled tongue. The chomper worked his incisors along the cob, and chewed with molars at the same time. His hunger increased the polite eating rate. "Boy, that was delicious. I'm having another one."

He repeated the performance with the second ear, and hurled the left-over cob as far as he could into the bushes. "Maybe just one more. Looks like you brought lots, May," he gleamed, as he grabbed another. As with the first pair, it too was soon somewhere off in the bushes lying amidst the leaves. "Boy, this stuff is just so good. How come you have such good corn, May?"

She didn't think that this year, or any year, her corn, was ever that special to have this kind of fuss made about it, but was friendly, "Probably just a good year. Lots of rain and sunshine."

"Either that or, you can really grow the stuff," replied Roy as he reached for another one.

"I see Roy couldn't wait." His brother came up from the river, where he too had gone for a quick dip, just to get refreshed, "I think you need something to go with that, Brother." Off Will trotted to the river to pull out three bottles of the twelve Bohemian Maid lager he'd put there earlier to cool, upstream, away from kidtraffic.

"You're right, just what I need to wash down this super corn," he said, as Will handed him one of the cool lagers, and he polished off cob number five. The salt on the corn encouraged thirst, so the first BoMaid sailed smoothly down his throat. "You should try some, it's really good."

"Maybe later." Will was used to the stuff, and, like all the farm folk, didn't see anything special about it, preferring to just coast away on the beer, without food. "Those kids sure are enjoying this," he observed.

"Yup," agreed Roy, as he put the empty bottle back on the case, and headed back to the corn pot.

"Gee whiz, you really do like that stuff," observed May. With the first couple of cobs, she'd figured he was just complimenting her out of soldier politeness.

"Like I said, May, this stuff is fabulous." He was beginning to run out of superlative adjectives.

The first child to notice how hungry all this water play made her, one of May's girls, arrived, "Mom, I'm hungry."

"I was expecting you," May smiled. "There's corn in the pot. But it's pretty hot. I'll get if for you."

Roy let the kid know, "It's darn fantastic corn, too, young lady. Your mom grows the best corn I've ever tasted. Can you pull one for me, too, May, while you're there."

May grabbed two, got them buttered, and gave both to her daughter, "Give one of them to Roy, Dear." The two corn comrades, sat together and munched away. "Tasty stuff, isn't it young lady?" said Roy.

"I guess so," replied the little one, half-heartedly, as she was so used to the stuff. In fact, she was almost sick of it, Mom had been boiling up so much of it lately.

Soon another child exited the river, out to the fire, rather than the water, because of exercise induced hunger. This one too retrieved a cob of corn, and one for Roy. "Thanks for bringing me a cob, there, young fellow," Roy thanked him.

"No problem. I guess you like this stuff, eh?" The youngster had watched Roy gnaw down the one before, and go on about the marvelous taste.

"Like it. Gawd, kid, I love it. Never ever had any like this before. It's, it's tremendfulous!" Roy gleamed.

"Oh," replied the lad, and moved away.

When the fifth hungry youngster came, and May directed him to the pot, he complained, "Mom, there's no more corn in here."

'That's okay," she replied, "there's plenty more where that came from. You, in fact, can help me by husking some of it. It's in that box over there", and she gestured to a box on the ground a few feet away.

"Okay, Mom," said the youngster, and he went to work shucking some more cobs, although he appeared not too happy about having been volunteered by his mother, just because he happened by at the wrong time.

The next kid to come along was hooked by the first laborer into helping, and within a few minutes, the pot was full again with about twenty fresh cobs of the yellow delight. May went over and threw in half a bag of fresh whole potatoes to cook alongside the cobs.

Roy yelled over at the workers, from his chair with the other two men, who were relaxing now, over beers, and just enjoying the day, and Roy's obsession, content with having finished haying for the season. "Let me know when this batch is ready so I can check it out."

"Boy, this guy wants to check everything, doesn't he?" commented one worker to the other.

As soon as the batch was done, they called to Roy, and he hustled over to check out the fresh batch, BoMaid in hand. He used the prong to grab out another one, and as before, munched it down. Then another. And another. "Gee, May, I just can't get over how deliciously fantastic this stuff is."

This time she responded, "Okay, Roy, I get it. The corn is good."

"Yup, it sure is," he smiled.

One of the kids, who had been observing Roy gobble down his last three cobs, looked at his cousin buddy, saying, "Boy, that guy is a bit strange. All he ever seems to do is eat corn."

"That's because he likes it," replied the cousin.

"Don't you think it's a bit strange?"

"Not really. I like corn. Don't you?" Roy had a defender of the corn faith.

"Well, yeah, but not like that guy."

"Maybe. But he's not one of those really crazy guys you hear about."

"No, not really bad," he said, hesitating, "I guess."

Finally Ellen had hamburgers ready, and yelled out to the whole party, "C'mon, everyone, all the grub is ready. Come and get it. Soup's on."

Within about a minute of the signal, the whole crew, those on land, and those still in water, had bunched around in a semi-wild throng, milling about, waiting for some sense of direction from Ellen. "Just get a plate over here, I'll serve you a burger, then go over there to Auntie, and she'll give you a nice fresh cob of corn. Okay, everyone? Little kids go first."

They all obeyed, especially the older adolescent types, and fell into line around the table where the hamburgers were ready, and then shuffled over to receive a cob of corn from May, who was standing by the pot, ready to dish one out to them. Just like in the army. After the first little kid got his fresh corn cob, May looked deeper into the pot, but alas, the corn was all gone. Only potatoes, boiled fresh potatoes. Hearty food, but nowhere near the taste of sweet succulent corn.

"Mom, Aunty said you'd give us corn, I want some corn," one of May's whined.

"Gee, there doesn't seem to be any left." May leaned over, and looked into the pot even closer. Sure enough, the pot held only potatoes. She looked up at the hungry line-up, apologetically, "Well, everyone, I guess all the corn is gone. You'll just have to do with potatoes."

A chorus of whining voices rang out immediately, all eight or so who had had none at all. Eventually the howling petered out, when the obvious fact became apparent to all of them: No more corn was going to be served at this feast. The grouchers, the grumpers, and the persistant, all had to be reminded of this true fact by the discouraged hostess, more than once.

May looked over at the empty bag under the table, and thought of Roy. She looked about for him, thinking that she'd like to give him a darn good scolding, if only he wasn't such a sargeant type, but he was nowhere to be seen.

"Where's Roy?" she called to the men.

"I saw him heading north through the bushes back towards the cars, a minute ago," called back Will. "I guess he needed to get something from his car."

Two of the persistant, now somewhat angry lads, too young to know any better, decided, even though Mom wouldn't like it, that they'd go find him, and give him heck on behalf of all the cornstarved children, poor hungry beggars.

They snuck off in the other direction to avoid being noticed, planning to circle the campfires, and catch up to Roy, wherever he was.

When they arrived back on the road, they spotted him walking along the trail beyond where the cars were, and began running to catch up. After having gone about a hundred yards, he had stopped. They approached with some caution, but by the time they got really close, he was keeled over, and was disgustingly returning his undue share of corn, mixed with some BoMaid, back to Mother Nature, in a huge yellowy pile. They stopped, too, as this was certainly not a time to give him heck. Fellas weren't that dumb.

One turned to the other. "Good thing we didn't eat any. Stuff must be poisonous somehow."

"Yup. Only poison could get you that sick." agreed the buddy.

Together they hustled back to share the good news to the fortunate cousins who had lucked out at not partaking.

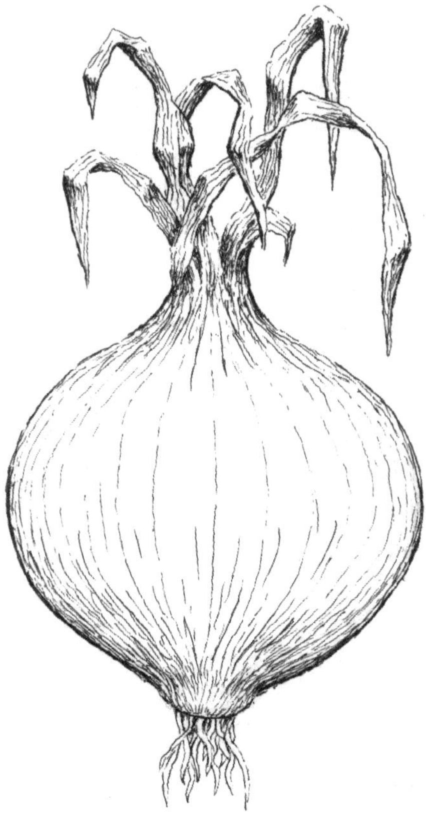

# The Onion

Twenty-five year old Pierre Lamarche was fed up with the lack of job opportunities in Montreal. "There is no future here for myself, unless I am to learn English. My modeling career will surely stop with the appearance of grey hair, and I will not use Grecian formula like that guy Maurice Richard." So the French Canadian chap decided to move west for a period, with a single purpose in mind: to learn English by way of cultural integration. Through a friend who had had the same difficulty, Pierre hit upon the ideal way to solve his problem: landing a beerslinger job in a busy local saloon some 15 miles south of the Battle.

Work at the hotel would provide daily interaction with English that would force the language upon him, yet be not overwhelming, as the owner of the hotel, and his wife, Marcel and Lily, were fluently bilingual. If Pierre were to encounter any linguistic difficulties, he could always count on Marcel or Lily to bail him out. In short, the conditions were ideal.

At the hotel where Pierre landed his job, there worked an Albertan chap, Jason, only nineteen, who knew absolutely no French, but was adventurous in spirit, and open to helping Pierre gain his English skills. Soon Pierre befriended the younger westerner. They slung beer, and were for two months, the hotel's main booze bringers. On days off, or before the evening's toil, with not a lot to do, at Jason's suggestion, the pair would slip out to the Battle to fish. This would benefit Pierre with his development of English, as fishing is a different environment than a bar, as well as provide some downtime from the hectic pace of bartending labor.

Pierre's French Canadian wit and lack of English skills, coupled with his natural French sex appeal, and charm, besides making for superior tips at the workplace, provided comic linguistic humour for the mostly unilingual Albertans who encountered him.

A thirsty customer would shout at him, "Pierre, bring me a Pilsener."

"One Pilsener, Boss," the happy French Canadian would call out to Marcel, who worked behind the bar.

"One Pil coming up, Pierre." Marcel would say, as he reached for the fridge.

Gracefully, as a Parisian fine waiter would, Pierre carried the single bottle of Pil over to the customer. In broken but understandable English, Pierre's voice would ring out, "Dat would be eighty cents, Boss." Everybody, each customer, Marcel, Lily, and all workers, Pierre called "Boss", as this name served every circumstance, as Pierre had trouble remembering all the English 'funnee' names.

Often, when first hearing an unfamiliar English name, he would, for humour, ask, "What kind of a name is dat? Neverr erd of such a name as dat." There just weren't enough Guys and Jacques for him. Too many hard to say, unfamiliar handles. So there were plenty of 'Bosses' around.

One particular chilly May day, the fishermen hooked up with Jason's Dad, who claimed he knew the fish-lucrative Battle holes, and could provide the information needed to catch more fish, which would have more relaxation, for the pair-become-trio. Upon setting out from town, Pierre looked at Jason, and predicted, "I theenk, Jaysawn, dat we will ave a good fishing time wit your fadder, no?"

Jason's father, because he wanted to demonstrate his knowledge, selected a secret hole, even though it was a long hike for him, quite out of the way, and far from any roads. The one hour hike was no problem for Jason or Pierre as they were used to much longer leg work each night, while bartending. Jason's father, though, would likely break a sweat, as long walks were not so customary for him.

The trio met at Jason's Dad's farm early, around 8 AM. It was a cool 5 degrees Celsius, so Jason's father made sure he dressed warm, with a couple of extra layers. Winter dress. "You guys are going to get cold," he warned the younger guys," as they jumped in the truck.

"It'll warm up soon enough, Dad," replied Jason.

It was 9 AM by the time they arrived at the 'special' spot, and Pierre, who had tremendous patience, casting again, and again, caught a walleye, and recognized it as different than the ones (pike) he and Jason had caught on earlier adventures. "Jaysahn, my friend, whaht kind of feesh is dis wahn?" he called, walleye still on hook.

"Pierre, that is called a pickerel," Jason responded.

"A pickereelll?" Pierre always wanted the correct sound.

"Yes, a pick - er - el." Jason pronounced it slower.

"Pickereelll?" Pierre said it again, with identical accent as the first time.

"You got it!" shouted Jason, congratulating his friend's quick learning of the name, and giving up on accent, knowing that part was about 20 times harder to teach than the sounds.

"You eat it?" Pierre questioned.

Jason answered, smacking his lips, "Yes, Pierre it is good to eat."

"Then I keep, non?" Pierre asked, wanting to know if they should keep it to eat

"Yes, Pierre, keep it," said Jason.

Pierre concluded the decision, and figured out what he could do. "Sokay, Jasawn, I wihll keep it. I will geeve it to Marcel at de bar."

Jason's father admired this, the fishing, the comraderie, the ongoing language, and his own contribution to the day. The morning sun had warmed the earth, and his only regret was the wearing of too much clothing. The young guys had been right.

There was new language in the fishing context, quite different from the familiar confines of the tavern, and Pierre was eager to have the opportunity. His vocabulary was growing quickly. He learned sounds easily, but the accent gave him trouble, as it does for anyone learning a fresh language. Linguistically, he kept the French system of accenting the last syllable more.

For now, there was little chat, and lots of fishing. Speaking occurred mostly only when Pierre wished to learn a new name of something, and his most common question was, "Jason, my friend, waht do you call dis?" while holding up the 'this' and Jason would help.

By noon, it was time to depart the hole, and Pierre had added an additional pickerel to his catch. Both Jason and Father had caught only rocks, which Pierre enjoyed, "I guess we know who is de betterh fisherman, eh, Jaysahn?"

"It's because those stupid pickerel probably understand French, Pierre. I heard you calling out to them." Jason claimed, in silly fisherman sour grapes.

Father, not to be outdone, added, "I saw you spitting that French spit of your's on the hooks, Pierre."

"You guys can cawmplain all you whant, but I ahm steel de best feesherman here," bragged Pierre.

The braggery continued all the way back along the trail, the trio walking much slower now, carrying the fish, and helping father with his parka, and other shed clothes. Upon arrival at the truck, father took off another sweater.

Pierre turned to Jason, and said, "Jasawnn, your fawdder is like an awnion."

"An onion?" queried Jason. He paused to think this over. This was confusing to the young Englishman. Did his Dad emit smell? Was he round? Was he attracting flies? How could Pierre see a similarity between an older man, and an onion? Onions must hold some sort of special significance in French Canadian culture. A simile the likes of he had never heard before. Not wanting to insult his father or embarrass Pierre in the truck, Jason mulled it over all the way to the farm. Perhaps Pierre was using some other word that sounded like 'onion', some French word.

When the trio turned back to a duo, Jason asked, "Uhh, Pierre, please explain what you meant, back there, when you said my dad is like an onion."

"You see, Jaysawn, your fawdder was peeling 'is skins, like an awnion." Pierre attempted to explain.

"You mean he's sunburned?" asked Jason.

"Sunburned? What you mean, Jaysawn, 'sunburned'?

Pierre was obviously not familiar with or did not understand 'sunburn', so Jason explained, "Sunburned is when the sun is so hot it burns your skin, so you get red and peel."

"Ha, ha. Noohh. Noohh. Dat is not what Pierre means. You see, Jaysawn, your fahdder is taking off his clohding, you know, like his coat, and his swehterr. Awnions have many skins, like dat, and he was taking off his many skins, juhst like an awnion. Now you uhnderstand, no?"

Jason, the linguistic dufus, finally clued in, "Yes, Pierre, Jason understands now. Ha ha. He is like the onion. Now, thanks to you, I will not be able to eat onions ever again. It will make me think I am a cannibal."

"Jaysahn, what you mean by cannibahl?" Pierre looked confused.

# The South of France

There is much more purpose to fishing than fishing itself. Fishing also means comraderie, and of course, feasting. A few weeks later, Jason and Pierre, now comrades by day, and beerslinging colleagues at night, returned to the same hole, sent there on a mission for the Boss, Marcel. Marcel and Lily owned the local hotel near the Battle, and were French immigrants from France, not Quebecois French. They had immigrated some twenty years back, to the west of Canada to establish the hotel business, and begin a fresh life. Family remained over in France, and now that Marcel's business was thriving, the couple returned once every two years or so. In their blood was French village mentality culture that was not to be removed that easily, certainly not by twenty years in a different culture. Whatever chance there was to 'return home' was looked upon as fortunate. So the thought of a fresh fish feast with friends was magnetic. It would substitute for the true thing, at one one-hundredth the cost

Marcel had planned it. “Tell, you what, boys. That pickerel you caught the other day was so tasty. You two should go out there again, and catch a few, this time, not just one or two. Then, before you go to work, Lily will fry them all up for supper in a traditional French way and we will have a fine French feast, over at my house. Pierre and Jason will both learn something of real French culture, eh, Pierre, and it shall be fun. You guys bring the fresh fish, I will supply the wine, and Lily shall cook. It will be a festive time. You both deserve it, you work so hard around here. It will be a small way I can show my gratitude.”

Hearing of Marcel’s plan, Pierre turned to Jason, “Sounds lahk a good idea, eh, Jaysawn?”

Jason agreed, “Yes, Pierre, it sounds like a good idea. I hope we can catch some fish.”

Pierre, being more confident in general, was more confident, also, of this idea. “No prohblemm. If da boss say we av to catch feesh, den we av to catch feesh, no?”

Jason figured he had to agree. “Okay, Pierre, you are the boss.”

Pierre did not at first understand Jason’s use of ‘boss’. So he disagreed, “No, no, Jaysawn, he is de boss,” pointing to Marcel.

Marcel, realizing he had errored in the proposition, that Jason might be right, there was no guarantee, altered his plan, “Tell you what, boys. Come back by about 4 o’clock or so, and if there are no fish, then so be it. Lily will go buy some, and we will still have the feast, okay. That way, all will be fine, anyway.”

Pierre admired Marcel’s decision. “You see, Jaysawn, dat is why dis guy is de boss, it’s becawz he know waht to do. See?”

“Yes, Pierre, I see,” agreed Jason, still skeptical of this fine plan, and not sure where it might lead. Certainly there was cultural doubts, as he guessed there would be plenty of food, and merriment, not something a nineteen year old mostly non-drinking fellow may be able to handle.

So the planned fantastic French cuisine feast day came along, and off the pair drove. And what do you know? Fisher God stayed close that day, and together the anglers caught exactly eight pan sized walleye, two for each person, and returned to the hotel to proudly announce their success, to Marcel.

“So fellows, did you catch any fish?” asked Marcel, curious if stage two of the plan could now go into effect.

Pierre, all smiles, announced proudly, “Oui, Marcel, togedder, we caught eight feesh. Waht do you wish us to do wit dem?”

Marcel who had the whole event preplanned, informed the still casually dressed fishermen, “Lily is here. She can take them home now, and you good fellows come over around six, and we will have the feast.”

Pierre was excited, “Jaysawn, I will have sleep, and den we can go over dair. It will be a fun time, no?”

"Yes, Pierre, I am looking forward to it, too," said Jason, who did not know what to expect, really, but what the heck. Can't live my life in Dullsville forever.

The appointed time arrived. The pair, now showered, and dressed for work, pulled up in Jason's car, and were warmly greeted by an apronned Lily, who proudly had cooked these fish in a French way, as if transported to her childhood of rural life in a pleasant valley of southern France.

She greeted them, pretending to be the French hostess/maid "Welcome, Gentlemen, come on in. The fish are almost ready. Marcel is waiting for you at the table."

Pierre accepted the cordial invite to enter the pretend humble cottage. "Tank you, Lily, Jaysawn and I are veree proud to be ere."

A smiling Marcel waited at the table, which was decked out in Lily's finest china and cutlery. "Welcome, my workers. First we shall have a toast to the fishermen. Let me give you each a glass of this fine French wine I bought for us today at the liquor store. If I would have known this event was going to happen, I would have brought back more wine from France last summer. However, this will have to do." He poured the entire contents into three large glasses, larger than Jason had ever seen.

So the three, a bonafide French goodfellow, a Quebecois French, and an English westerner with no clue of the proper behavior, put together by fate, partook of the wine, honoring Marcel's proud way of the French. "How are the fish coming, Lily, my sweet?" Marcel called out.

From the kitchen, Lily responded, "Marcel, they are almost ready. In about another ten minutes."

Marcel, true to his word, continued, "Well, my fine fishermen friends. I suppose we shall open another bottle while we wait," and he left the table to retrieve another 'fine' bottle of vintage, again of the liquor store variety. He expertly uncorked it, as though he could have done it blindfolded, and refilled the now empty glasses.

"Okay, the fish are ready now. I am bringing them in." Lily proudly announced. The three fellows, having embellished their desire for food, from wine, awaited anxiously, eager to compliment the wine with freshly cooked fish. Not just any fish, but walleye, reputedly the tastiest variety in all of Canada, perhaps the world.

Marcel charmed his wife, "Ah, Lily, they look just beautiful, fried up in lots of butter, not filleted. This will surely be a feast no one will forget. It reminds me so much of home. But, you know, fish is not meant to be eaten without some fine white wine. I think we should have another bottle." He excused himself to retrieve it, and this time split it equally into four glasses, as he included Lily into the gathering.

Jason, by now, was feeling the alcohol's effects, as drinking this much wine may have been the custom in France, but not in rural Alberta. Beer was more to Jason's liking. Pierre was fairing only slightly better, as he too was not a daily wine partaker. Marcel seemed totally normal.

Jason, unsure, expressed some doubt of the circumstance, "You know, Marcel, Pierre and I have to get back to the bar by seven to work. Perhaps I should go easy on the wine."

Marcel disagreed, "Oh no, Jason, you are a fine worker, and I am the boss. If I can't let you work at my place with some wine in you, then who can?"

Pierre, who was more familiar with the ways of Marcel, as he had worked for Marcel substantially longer, spoke up, "Oui, Jaysawn, mah feesherman friend, Boss knows what 'e is doeeng. Drink up! Relax! You may nevair 'ave anodder chance like dis wahn. Beside, I ahm wit you, no?"

Jason could not disagree, "Yes, Pierre, that is true. I just want to be able to work."

Marcel was listening, but seemed to have no care for the matter, "I think now that this matter is clear, we should celebrate with another bottle. Lily, do you think you could find us another bottle?"

"Yes, of course, Marcel," Lily, ever the French hostess, retrieved another fine white wine, a different variety again. Jason watched, and showed mild dissatisfaction, which Marcel read.

He turned again to Jason. "Thank, you, my dear. You see, Jason, in France we never eat without fine wine. This particular bottle is one that I did bring back from France last summer, it is one of the most superior of it's kind in all of France, and you have a chance to drink up, so drink up. Perhaps this will be your only chance, no? So be merry. Do not spoil the occasion with a sour face."

Jason, feeling more and more liberated from his narrow viewpoint, mostly due to alcohol induced restructuring of thoughts, nodded, "Okay. You are the boss."

"That's for sure. I am the boss." Marcel smiled.

"Dat's for sure, Jaysawn, 'e is de boss," Pierre seconded the notion.

Having given in now to this cultural tradition, and realizing he had no polite way of backing out, Jason joined in wholeheartedly. In his dislogic from the wine, he began to partake at the very same rate as Marcel, outdoing even Pierre, at the tasting, pouring, guzzling traditions that were being shown him, so courteously by the gracious host, and hostess. A slurp of wine accompanied each morsel of fish down each of the four throats. There was a lot of fish.

Eventually the Battle River delights, tasty walleye that they were, buttered and browned to perfection, were all devoured, and the four people, two of them much richer from the experience, sat back, and just relaxed, stuffed from the delectable feast. Rich ceremonial customs of France had travelled to Alberta via the lovely couple. Eleven empty bottles of white vintage were sporadically scattered amidst the now messed fine china, proof that a remarkable feast had just occurred. Jason, unaccustomed to all this fuss over a meal, felt overwhelmed by the hospitality, the food, and the wine. "Dat was exshellent, Marcel. I tank you, and Lily, of course. Tank you. Tank you bote."

Marcel spoke. "There is only one more tradition, Jason, that you have not partaken of. We have about twenty more minutes before you two have to get to work. No French meal like this would be right if we did not have some fine Cognac to wash down the fish, and get that aftertaste out of your mouth. Have you ever tasted cognac?

Jason only knew that it was some kind of booze. "Acshoolly, no, Marcel, I have not. What is it?"

Well then, this is your first chance, my friend. I will be the one to initiate you to such a tradition. Next to wine, Cognac is France's favorite drink. The cognac I brought back from home last summer has never been opened. I could not think of a more appropriate occasion than this, no?"

Jason looked on with drunken curiosity. "Whatever you say, Boss. Whatever you say. Pierre, what do you think?"

Pierre encouraged his friend. "Jaysawn, if he is de boss, then he is de **BOSS**, when are you everh goeeng to learn that wahn? Eh, Jaysawn? You should always do what de boss says you should do. Right, Marcel? Besides, it will make you feel bettair before going to work, no?"

Marcel added. "Pierre has it correct, Jason. Drink up. It is my problem if you cannot work, not yours. Lily, do you have the Cognac? Jason, I will explain to you the correct way to drink Cognac. You take the glass like this, see, and then you pour it all down at once." Marcel put the glass to his lips, gave it one sound sniff, and poured it back his oh so dry eager French throat. "You see, Jason, that is the way it is done. See?"

"Yes, boss. I see," said Jason, having only in part seen the process.

"Then you shall have one, no?"

"Yes, boss, I will have one." Marcel had it already poured.

"And Pierre?" he said, handing another to the Quebecois.

"Oui, Boss. Of course Pierre will take the fine cognac. One cannot get it like theese in Quebec, no?"

"And one more for the both of you, for good measure. It will make your evening happier." With mastered liquor serving technique, he took back their glasses and refilled each to the line.

"Yes, Boss." Jason rolled his eyes in disbelief, and fear, of the upcoming evening, going to work this hammered.

"Oui, Boss." agreed Pierre, looking over at Jason, he too pondering how the evening would go, for each of them. "To not have would be sacrilegious, no?" They each drank the second one, with Pierre telling Marcel how it was lovely, and Jason grimacing, as with the first one.

The time to leave was at hand. Marcel announced the feast's end. "Lily, I think it is time now for my two young workers here to be off to work. It is too bad we cannot continue. I myself am feeling a bit tired out with all your fine cooking, sweetheart."

"Yes, Marcel, it is time they were off to work," Lily agreed.

Jason and Pierre, each in his own turn, thanked Lily again for the wonderful meal, said, "Au revoir, for now," to Marcel and stumbled their tipsy bodies to the car. Jason, with the car windows wide open, managed somehow to drive himself and his Quebecois friend to work.

The tavern was much more active than usual upon their arrival. They put on the aprons immediately, and got down to work, winging trays of beer to the tables. Pierre's happy mood encouraged tipping from the amorous females, as well as the regular folk, who didn't normally see him this way. His mind clicked into bartender mode, and he easily remembered orders, and prices. When a bartender has been drinking, some drinkers see a comraderie there, and tip because of it.

Jason was not faring so well. The first order was for two Blue, but by the time Jason got to the counter to retrieve, he had forgotten, and took back two Pilsener instead. The customer looked at him, "We ordered Blue, young man. We don't want these." Jason returned them, and got two Molson Canadian, so the customers gave in, and purchased those, but did not look impressed.

And so the evening wore on, Pierre doing a better job than normal, and Jason totally messing things up. By nine o'clock, he had spilled draft on a lady, given several rum and cokes instead of rye and cokes, and told Larry, the behind the counter guy, that several people wanted fine white wine, or cognac. Fortunately for the regular folk, the bar was split into two sections for serving, so most of the people at Jason's end had moved down to Pierre's end, where they could at least get what they ordered. Those who could not read the situation had exited, in search of better service.

With only one poor fellow remaining in his end, Jason sat down for a break. He watched Pierre work the tables, cracking jokes, teasing females, doing balancing tricks with beer, and buying sporadic free rounds. Gratuitous money flowed to his tray from the hands, in exchange for the entertainment. "A lot better than a stripper!" a guy yelled out.

Pierre smiled at Jason, as he called a complex order to Larry. "You don't look too appy, my good friend. What is wrong?"

"I'm tired, Pierre. My feet are sore." Jason did not return the smile.

"Well, then, why don't you just take dose shoes off, and relax? I can handle all de work. Look, if you feel bad wit de shoes off, I will take mine off as well." Pierre seated himself beside Jason, and pulled off his own shoes and socks. Jason just stared, in an uncaring stupor.

When Larry called, "Pierre, this order is ready," Pierre bounced back to his feet, now barefoot, and took off to make deliveries, and to entertain some more, the bare feet just inducing more tipping from the laughing customers.

Jason watched for a moment, and then felt, from his belly, a need to get somewhere. He strode a twisting path through the delivery door at the back, to the fresh air, and to the large garbage cans. Fortunately for him, the first one was empty. Within ten minutes, so was his stomach, the walleye having escaped, accompanied by a quantity of wine, and cognac. Jason crawled to the nearby wall and propped himself up, ready for the next round of heaves, should it decide to involuntarily come up. He muttered, "Better me out here, than in there, anyway," and nodded off.

Not until after last call at 12 did Pierre notice Jason was gone. He and Larry searched, eventually discovering Jason's slumped body. They retrieved some ice from the ice box, wiped it over Jason's face, and together brought him back inside, cleaned him up, and put him back on a chair beside the bar. Larry made some coffee, and Pierre joined his fisherman friend.

Marcel showed up at 12:30, feeling much rested, as resting had been his only boss duty for the evening. Being the boss had such wonderful bonuses.

He joined the pair at their table, "Well, my good fisherman friends, how did the evening go?"

Jason, looking ghostly, lied, "Fine, Boss, fine."

Pierre, himself appearing just plain tired, agreed, "Oui, Boss, Jaysawn is right, de evening, she went fine."

"Yes, fellows, I knew it would. With such a good start, how could it not go well, eh?" Then Marcel stood up to start helping Larry with the cleanup.

The cheerful Quebecois turned to wink tiredly at Jason, "What Boss not know not hurt him, eh, Jaysawn? We shall go fishing tomorrow, no?"

# The Cowboy Hat

Surely over the years many a strange thing has floated along the Battle: Discarded furniture from people so blind they can't distinguish between garbage sites and rivers, bottles with poorly written notes from dreamy children, and perhaps corpses, the results of murders or accidents. Rivers are wondrous things in their ability to dispose. By the time the water flows around the next corner, the story behind the item, may too be gone. One such item was a new, almost, anyway, cowboy hat. How it arrived on the waters of the Battle is a long tale.

Henry Desjardin, his older brother Paul, and friend Denys were desperate for summer work. At home on the Metis Settlement, there was no work, and they were bored. Out of school, aged sixteen and seventeen, the young men needed to leave.

Dad said, "Henry and Paul, it's time for you boys to move out of here. You should go away, go south to where there are farmers, where you can get some work on a farm or something, okay. I don't want you hanging around here all summer."

Paul and Henry figured this was a helluvan idea. No money here. Might as well get a job. Any pay was better than here. "Can we have the car for a couple of days, then?" Paul asked.

"Sure," replied Dad, hoping to get rid of them for at least the summer, and hoping also that they could break out of this place, into the world of whites, where perhaps a better future lied. "Take it tomorrow. Go to Vermilion. Perhaps there is work there. Ask the farmers." Advice they would heed, for they didn't know what else, or how else to do it, to begin the transition into independence.

That evening the brothers visited Denys, "Hey, tomorrow we are taking Dad's car to Vermilion. We're getting jobs. You want to come?"

"Sure," replied Denys, what kind of job do you have?"

Paul made it clearer. "Oh, we don't have jobs. Dad wants us to go be farmers. He said we could find work in Vermilion. You want to come?"

"Sure, said Denys. He had nothing to lose.

Denys came over bright and early the next morning. "You guys still going to Vermilion?" he looked at them unsure, as these friends often changed their minds about these things, often not getting the guts, preferring to stay home, safe.

"Of course. We're getting jobs, remember?" said Paul, looking at his friend as though Denys should have realized they were serious all along.

"Well, then. Let's go." Denys, at least, was ready.

At the gas tank, Dad gave them some last minute advice. "Paul, you drive the car careful. I need it back tonight, or tomorrow. Soon. Somebody has to bring it back when you get jobs. Lots of gas for there and back. You will need some money for food, and maybe a hotel room for the night. Be careful. Vermilion is a big town." He gave Paul a ten dollar bill, trusting the eldest, and most mature, at least in his eyes, to take charge. "Take care of your brother, and good luck."

Henry looked one more time at the old house, and his Dad, this being his first time out on such adventure. In fact, it would be his first trip to Vermilion. The worst that could happen was a day in a strange new town with friends. "Don't worry, Dad, I will take care of *him*." He smiled, his sixteen year old face lighting up, at the prospect of taking charge of his older brother and Denys, the good natured but equally irresponsible friend.

The trio of would be farmers set out in the '56 rusted Chevy, all optimistic yet frightened. "Wow, ten dollars. If we don't get jobs, we can spend the money, eh?" Paul was not too keen on actually getting a job, but at least they had to go try. Enough to have a story or two for Dad about how hard it had been, when they got home that night, or the next day.

"So what are we gonna do when we get to Vermilion?" queried Denys, figuring the brothers would have a plan.

"We're gonna get jobs. We told you that before." Paul wondered if Denys could hear.

"No, Paul, I think he means what are we gonna do when we *get* to Vermilion." Henry was smarter. "What are we exactly going to do?"

"We're going to go to outside the bar, and ask people there where the jobs are," Paul replied, himself having a plan, even if the other two didn't. "Then when there are no jobs, we can get some guy to buy us a case of beer."

Henry was a bit more serious about doing as his father had said, "If we go to the bar, they'll think we're just looking for booze, not jobs. That's a dumb idea. We should stand outside the grocery store."

Paul didn't really like the idea of Henry making sense. "Denys, what do you think? Should we go outside a bar, or outside a dumb grocery store?"

Denys didn't care. Mostly he was just along for the ride. "I don't care. You guys decide."

"How about we flip a coin, then?" suggested Paul.

"I think we should just drive by both places, and see which one has the most likely looking people at it," Henry figured this would prove himself right.

"But if we go to the bar, people there will be much friendlier, eh? Maybe if they are drunk, they will be more likely to hire us." Paul was determined to get as close to the bar as possible, for when the time came that they gave up on finding jobs.

They continued the debate off and on all the way. At least it gave them a topic for conversation. Upon arrival in town, Paul drove around until he spotted a 'HOTEL' sign. "There it is. We should park around the corner, so they won't see the car. They'll think we're Indians if they see the car."

Henry interjected, still disputing this theory of hotel being better than store, "Keep driving until we see a grocery store. There's nobody here outside the hotel. There will be lots of farmers buying groceries today."

Paul finally gave in, in part, "Okay, Henry, tell you what, we'll try over there for an hour or so, just because you want to. Then after that we go to where I say, okay?"

Henry was totally satisfied with this, at least there would be a chance. Unlike his brother, he did at least partially want a job. Paul parked the car about a block away from the grocery, and got out. "Let's go then. Go find a job."

"Yup, Paul. Go find a job," said Denys, showing confidence in his friend.

Henry was nervous. "What do we say to people?"

Paul loved it when Henry seeked advice. "Its easy. You just say. 'Excuse me, Mister, but do you have any work? We're looking for work.' something like that, anyways."

"How do we know which guys are farmers? What if we ask someone who ain't a farmer?" Henry needed to have a wiser, more likely to succeed, plan.

"If he isn't a farmer, he won't hire you, eh? Won't hurt to ask, anyway," answered Paul.

"Okay, then who is going to ask? The three of us can't all talk together at the same time." Henry continued.

"I will, o' course," said Paul, knowing it was his job, he being the eldest and all.

"Okay. Say the right thing," advised Henry.

The threesome stood beside the exit door, where every shopper would have to pass them. The first person to exit was an elderly woman. "She's not a farmer," whispered Henry, to his brother.

"How do you know?" asked Paul.

"Guess I don't for sure. Ask her if you want to." Henry was uncomfortable.

"If she's a farmer?" Paul didn't know if Henry was saying to ask her if she was a farmer, of if she had jobs.

"If she's a farmer," Henry clarified.

"There's no point asking her then. Let's wait until we see someone who we know is a farmer." By this time the lady had passed by already, and had only given them a brief distrusting stare.

"Well, you really messed up that one, Paul," declared Henry.

"She weren't no farmer. I'll get the next one. It's gotta be a man. Them're the only ones who can hire us anyway."

Burns, a farmer from twenty miles south, walked out next. This time the farmer look was apparent. Farm boots. Farm coveralls. Farm jacket. As he walked by them, he nodded a 'hello' in their direction.

"Hey, Mister, got a minute?" Paul was able to get Burns to stop.

"What do you want?" Burns was to the point.

"We were wondering if you need any help on your farm. We're looking for a job." Paul spoke for all three.

Burns did need someone, but he wasn't sure if any one of these guys was exactly what he was looking for. He'd heard of two problems with hiring Metis youth. The first was that the guy may not be capable, from laziness, or lack of skill, or inability to learn. He might also take off after the first payday, and you'd just have to find a replacement. The second problem was that a young kid needs his peers. Friends of the fellow would be hanging around, at least on weekends, to share in the pay, or just have some fun. Burns didn't need any of those kinds of problems. Yet he could use a fellow. Perhaps, just perhaps, one of these young fellows might be very trainable, hard working, and might even come back the following summer, if you treated him right. It was worth a shot. Besides, after a couple of days, if it wasn't working out, you could just pay him and take him back to town. It wouldn't cost much, as these guys would work for a bit less than the going rate. They probably didn't even know the going rate. "Well, first of all, I only need one person. I don't need three. You're not all looking for a job together, are you?"

"Nope. We just all want jobs. We can split up." replied Paul.

"Well, I'll take one of you, just for a couple of days, though." Burns didn't want to hurt the young man's feelings somewhere down the road, if he had to let him go. This way the fellow would at least figure he'd lived up to the whole contract, and there would be no hard feelings. In fact, although he was secretive about it, Burns could probably put someone to work right through harvest.

"Hey. That's good." Paul looked over at Henry. "I told you we'd get jobs."

"So which one of you is coming with me? You can come right now. Start today." Burns didn't make many trips to town, and figured these guys were probably without transportation, so the easiest thing for him was just to take the new hired hand home, now.

The three young men looked at each other. This was something they hadn't expected, or even wanted. To dream of getting a job, and now to be actually getting one, were two different stories. Mostly they were just here to please

Dad, and maybe have a fun time with a case of beer. This event had disrupted the real plans. Paul looked at Burns. "For sure you want somebody today? Couldn't start tomorrow?"

"Nope. Today." replied Burns, clearly, figuring if the guy promised to show up tomorrow, most likely he wouldn't, or couldn't, for the lack of transportation. And, he sure didn't want to drive the twenty miles back to town on just the verbal promise. That would be a trip for nothing, a long shot at best.

"Counts me out. Dad wants his car back tonight, or tomorrow." Paul was relieved to have such a good excuse.

"Me or Denys could drive it home," argued Henry.

"Nope. Dad gave it to me to take care of." Paul didn't want the job. "This job is between you and Denys. I'll get a better one anyway."

Burns had been watching, and listening, but didn't see a decision arriving quickly, and figured they might not actually even want to work. "My truck is that blue one over there. I'll be waiting for five minutes. Whichever one of you who wants to come should be there, or I'm just driving away. Okay?"

"Sure," said Paul. "One of us will be over there right away." Then he turned to Denys, and Henry. "Well, how we gonna decide?"

Henry spoke. "I don't think that you even want the job. Don't know about Denys. He probably wants to stay with you. So I guess the job is mine, if I want it."

"Hey, how come you think I don't want a job. We all came here looking for jobs, didn't we? This one may not be my job, but that doesn't mean I don't want one." Paul didn't like his brother insulting his jobhunting integrity.

"Let's flip coins then, and the odd man out gets the job," suggested Henry.

Denys didn't like this idea. He might win, and have to go off with the farmer stranger, Burns, and have to work, and be without his friends. "Nope, that's a dumb idea. The guy who goes should be the one that wants the job the most. That's not me. I want a better job. Besides, we should have fun tonight celebrating that we got jobs. If one of us goes with that guy, he won't be able to party. That'd be too bad for him."

Burns started his truck, and revved it a bit, loud enough for them to hear, as a last warning to hurry up.

"Geez, see. That guy can't even wait. I sure wouldn't want to work for a guy like that, anyway." Paul had more excuses.

"Okay, then. That does it. I'm going." Henry had made the choice. To him, this was a no lose situation. He figured that Burns was probably a decent enough guy, and didn't think that Burns had meant the job was only two days long. He figured Burns was bluffing about that, although Paul and Denys probably hadn't figured it out. The worst would be that it lasted two days, and then he'd have to hitchhike or bus home. If that was the case, he could stay in Vermilion for the day and ask for jobs himself, which would be better than with all three of them together, anyway. He turned to his brother, and said, "Tell Dad

I'll be home soon," and trotted over to the truck, jumping in the passenger side.

"I'm Burns. I'm glad one of you decided to come." Burns stuck out his hand.

Henry shook it, with some youthful trepidation, the first time he had ever done anything so brave. "I'm Henry. Henry Desjardin." He was broke, only carrying what he was wearing, and scared. Burns scanned his clothing, especially the worn shoes, and realized he'd have to lend this young fellow work clothes, for now.

The job lasted more than two days. It didn't take Burns long to figure out he had made a steal. The first day was spent fencing, and Henry outworked Burns, easily, pounding in more fenceposts than Burns had ever seen pounded in a day, so much that by suppertime, Burns offered him the job for as long as there was work, which meant until the end of harvest.

The kid was intelligent, so learned machinery easily, was friendly, after the first day jitters, so got along with Burns' kids and wife, and had proven his strength. And he was willing to work the long hours for a mere $5 a day plus room and board. It took a week or so to settle in, which meant Henry had to make the weekend trip home for clothes, and of course, to bug Paul and Denys about his having a job, and they not. Burns dropped him off in Vermilion on Saturday afternoons, and picked him up Monday mornings, at the bus depot.

The summer flew by, and when harvest was over, Henry agreed to phone Burns the first week of May to see if he needed anyone for next year.

Henry phoned on the first of May, and the arrangement started up again. Burns was overwhelmed with his luck, that he'd made the right decision a year earlier. This year he didn't have to go looking for farm help, having to take pot luck off the street. Instead, one, and a damn good one, dropped right by, with no effort at all on Burns' part.

Henry's routine, of working five and a half days, and getting one and a half off, and getting a lift to and from town, proceeded normally until, one Saturday morning, the weekend of the Wainwright Stampede, when Henry spoke to Burns, "You don't need to take me to Vermilion today. My brother and his friend are going to pick me up. We're going to Wainwright to see the cowboys. They'll drop me off on their way back home tomorrow."

This suited Burns fine, as it would save him two trips to town. "Okay. I hope you and your friends have fun. Don't drink too much. That damn Stampede can get a little wild, you know." Burns treated Henry a bit like he was his own son. Their relationship had gone beyond employer/employee, and now bordered on friendship or father/son, at least in the off-time. Henry had fit in extremely well, spending time watching TV with the kids, while they bugged him by pulling out the occasional whisker on the up and coming beard. He played catch with the boys, and helped with parenting, a surrogate big brother, living and working as a family member would.

After dinner, which was when Henry got off, he waited impatiently on Burns' step for the sound of his Dad's car, hoping these idiots would be true to their word, a word given the weekend before. The thirty dollars in his pocket seemed eager to be taken out.

Burns came up from his barn and asked, "Are you sure they're coming. I could give you a ride to town anyway, you know."

"Oh, they'll be along. They're always late. Sometimes they get a bit slow." What he really meant was sometimes they get drunk too soon in the day on Saturdays, but he didn't want Burns to know that.

Burns smiled, suspecting what 'slow' had really meant, but not letting on. "Well, just come and get me, when you want. Anytime today. If it gets to tomorrow, you might as well stay for the weekend. Maybe tomorrow you can come fishing with me and the kids."

The prospect of 'becoming' a Burns, even for a single full off day, did not sit well with Henry. His identity as a Metis would be challenged. Up to now he was farmer for five and a half days, and then Metis teenager having fun for a day and a half. The two cultures collided, and so far he had been able to keep both well and alive, just as he wanted. He just sat and hoped those two goofs would be along soon, even though this year they were less of goofs, having each landed jobs of their own, closer to home, and for less money than his, but jobs still.

Around three in the afternoon, he heard the unmistakable sound of the '56 Chevy. His brother Paul drove up the driveway, and spun the car around so he wouldn't have to get out of the car when he talked to Henry, "You ready?" he called.

"Yup," answered Henry, being that he had sat there waiting for just over three hours, being 'ready'. He wanted to give Paul hell about it but decided that a sibling fight would be a dumb way to start the day. He crawled past Paul into the back seat, greeting Denys on the way in.

Paul gunned the car, and spun a bit on the way out. The rumble would at least let Burns know that Henry's friends had come for him.

Henry was smiling at the prospect of a relaxing childlike, yet crazy day with his buddies, something he hadn't done in a while. Fun weekend. Still, he wanted to know why they were late. "How come you weren't here at noon?"

"We stopped in Vermilion, and got us a six pack," smiled Denys, as he handed an open one to Henry.

"It took you three hours to get a case of beer?" Henry asked, in disbelief, wondering why it would take them that long.

Paul explained it. "First we went into the bar, but the guy asked us how old we were, so we had to leave. Then it took us a long time to find someone to buy it for us. We were strangers, eh?"

"So how come you didn't get the guy to buy you more than just a six-pack, because now, if we want more beer, we'll have to find someone else in Wainwright?" Henry liked explanations.

"Well, we spent all the money on gas, and that's all the money we had. Enough only for one six-pack. How much money do you have?" answered Paul.

"Thirty bucks. Plenty enough to do us." As always, Henry's money became everyone's money. Just as Paul's money or Denys's money was everyone's money. The ownership of cash was always the group's, whether it was the family, or the peers. That's just the way it was. The only control Henry would have was that he could carry it. Any purchase would be the decision of the group. This was a Metis youth custom he loved, as whenever *he* was broke, someone else usually had some to share. It always seemed to even out, although no one kept track at all.

By the time the three eager hombres arrived in Wainwright, transformed temporarily into a hustling town because of the Rodeo, they had warmed up from the beer. Henry had been to the place with Burns a few times, so he navigated from the back seat. "There are two bars, downtown, but first we should just drive around for awhile so we can see where the rodeo is."

Paul drove around, down streets, back alleys, and avenues, following directions from the passengers, until they got a sense for the place. It was a sense of friendliness, and celebration, from the once a year event. In the afternoon sunshine, they noticed all the people were smiling, and jubilant. Paul honked the horn at some girls, who ignored Denys's friendly wave. Soon they had done two tours of Main Street, and had discovered where the rodeo grounds were, by following the traffic flow.

"Boy, everyone here looks like they're going to the rodeo. Look at those cowboy hats. They all got one on. We better buy us some because we'll look out of place if we don't," said Denys.

"That's for sure. Let's find a store and get us some," agreed Paul. He parked the Chevy beside a department store, close to the hotels.

The trio of soon to be cowboys strolled confidently into the store, and gazed around until they found the cowboy hats, a varied collection of the nation's finest stetsons and the like.

"Wow, look at these." Denys picked the nearest one off the shelf and put it atop his head, and it fell down to his ears, oversized. "I'm a cowboy now, eh." He beamed proudly at the brothers, obviously transformed in two seconds, into a character he had never been before. One that could ride a horse, or rope a calf, or at least it appeared he could.

"Yup, you're a cowboy now, Denys. An injun cowboy." Paul adored the new look Denys, and grabbed a white one off the shelf for himself. His fit better, and he joined the newly found cowboyhood. "Me, too. Call me Big Paul, the cowboy."

Henry, feeling excluded from the cowboy organization, reached for one as well. "I am Little Henry, but tougher than Big Paul."

They took turns trying on several hats, admiring each other, and themselves, in the mirror. "Have we all decided yet?" asked Paul.

Henry, who had noticed the price on the hats, and had done some thinking, as well as trying on, spoke, "I don't know about this, don't you think we should save some of our money for later. Maybe we'll need some for out at the rodeo, or for food. These things are expensive. We only have thirty bucks."

"Henry's right, Paul," added Denys. "If we buy these hats now, we'll only have a few bucks left for the rest. Let's see. Seven dollars each is twenty-one bucks. That would give us only nine bucks for the rest of the day. Maybe we'll need gas to get home, too."

Paul realized they were right, but still, the wearing of hats did summon a severe personality change, out of kid Metis, and into adult Cowboys. He'd felt it, and so had his companions. "Maybe we could just buy one then, and at least we can take turns being cowboys. We can share it throughout the day," he suggested.

"That's a good idea," agreed Denys. "I think we should get the one I have. It's the nicest." He was mostly jesting, but part serious, hoping to get the one that at least fit him.

"We should get the one I picked out because I'm the oldest, and the driver," said Paul.

Henry corrected Denys. "No, we will get the one I picked out. I have the money in my pocket, remember. We should just get the cheapest one, and share it, like you said before," said Henry. "I like that idea."

Paul spoke, as the older tougher wiser brother. "Oh, don't tell us all about who's carrying the money. Money is to be shared with family and friends. If I had the money, it would be all three of ours. Denys and me could take you outside, and take all that money away from you, anyway. Then we could buy ourselves two hats. Besides, who says we even need hats?"

"Well, then I get to wear it first." Denys figured by saying that he would have first rights, if they did buy a hat.

"No, I get to wear it first," argued Paul, 'cause I'm the oldest."

"But if it's me whose paying for it, I get to decide who wears it, and I'm gonna wear it first." Henry tried to sound tough.

"Okay, Paul, then just how are we going to decide, then?" asked Denys.

"Well, I've already decided. I don't want a hat at all. It's stupid. This whole hat idea was stupid. Let's just forget it. Gotta save the money for later, for the rodeo, or for beer." Paul proceeded outside, having decided, not wishing any more silly arguing over hats.

Denys, who usually took Paul's lead, followed, leaving Henry by himself holding the hat he'd selected. Money in pocket, hat in hand, and argumentative buddies gone outside. What was he to do? No brainer. He proceeded to the counter, and spoke to the clerk. "I want this one."

"That'll be seven dollars." The clerk punched the till.

Henry gave her a ten, got back his three, then proudly, hat atop his head, walked briskly outside to face his friends. "I bought one for all three of us," he informed them.

"Well, that was pretty stupid, I guess. Now we only have a bit of money left for beer, and food, and rodeo." Paul looked unimpressed.

Denys grabbed the hat off of Henry's head, saying, "Then it's my turn to wear it, eh?" and put it on. It was too large, but that didn't matter. He had a cowboy hat.

"Fine guys, just fine. Let's go have a beer." Paul for now wanted nothing to do with the hat, or any fighting that might come of it. He headed directly to the nearby hotel, Denys and Henry following close behind, swung open the door, swaggered along to a table, and sat, reeking in pretend overconfidence, which wasn't much.

The bartender approached their table, "Need to see your IDs, guys."

"I don't have mine with me, but I'm 21. Ask my brother here." Denys had heard somewhere that sometimes this worked, if maybe the bartender was stupid. Might as well try, anyway, he figured. It didn't work. The bartender just stood his ground, saying, "Sorry, guys. I'm going to have to ask all three of you to leave."

"Well, this ain't a very friendly place, guess we'll just take our money elsewhere," Paul spoke emphatically, real angry like, and stood defiantly, as though he were ready to beat the tar out of this stupid bartender. On the way out he turned to Denys, and grabbed the hat, "Give it to me. You look older without it. Maybe if Henry wouldn't have been with us. He looks too young."

The bartender smiled in appreciation, as he watched them leave, entertained momentarily, by their collective youthful enthusiasm.

Outside the door, they huddled to discuss the next adventure. Paul kept advising, "Don't figure we'll get into the other hotel, either. I say we go to the rodeo, then come back here later, and find someone to buy us the beer. Then tonight we can go drink it."

Off to the Chevy, and along the road to the rodeo grounds they drove, still all enthusiastic. The day was young, and so were they. You don't need to be 21 to lose money on a midway. The gate admission was only a dollar each, a real bargain, so they strolled along, laughed at nauseous kids getting off rides, and jiggling to midway music. Heaven compared to home. "Well, you guys want to go to the rodeo, or should we just wander the midway?" asked Paul.

Henry looked over by the rodeo grandstand, observing, "Looks like the rodeo is over. All those people are coming out. Might as well stay here, and see what we can get into."

A carnival attendant beneath a sign saying, "Crown and Anchor" yelled out at them. "Hey, boys, come over here. Win some big money."

Henry grabbed the hat. "Gimme the lucky hat. Win some money. Then we can go back to the store, and buy two more hats. More money, more beer, too.

"Good plan, Henry," said Denys, as they heeded the beckoning call of the crown and anchor runner, "then we won't be fighting over it."

It took all of five minutes for each of them, each with the lucky hat upon his head, to lose a dollar each, a quarter at a time. "Don't think this hat is so lucky," grumped Paul. "Better try your luck without it." Five more minutes, each without the unlucky hat, and the Henry's wallet was thinner by three more dollars.

"Well, darn, Henry, look what you've done." Paul blamed his brother.

"I guess we're all just unlucky. Let's just not play this game anymore. Let's go win one of those big Teddy bears. You can take it back to Mom." They moved across the midway lane to the other side, to a baseball throwing, booth, where the object was to break the bottles on the planks.

The hypnotic preacher like voice echoed across enticingly, "Three shots for a quartah! Step right up, fellows! Strong guys like you can do it easy." They stepped right up, and some more cash disappeared, but not without laughs at how silly Paul's windup was.

"He looks like a he's throwing a spear. Even if he did hit a bottle, it wouldn't break," Paul whispered to Henry, as they watched, and heard the "Damn!", when the ball sailed over the whole arrangement of bottles and whomped into the canvas behind. The hat played musical heads as each took it off in order to throw.

A realization that this was not their game led them to wander further down the lane between rows of other tented skill competitions, able, from their losing, to ignore most of the enticing calls of the carnies, except for two more that appeared deceptively easy, but weren't, just as the bottle breaking one wasn't, until they arrived at the competition of hitting a rubber peg with a huge sledge hammer, to ring a bell on the tower above. "I can do that one," claimed Henry, "I've been practicing a lot, fencing with Burns."

"Bet you can't," claimed Paul. "I'll get closer to making the bell ring than you will."

"We'll see." Henry took the hat off, gave it to Denys, paid the man a quarter, and stepped right up. He took a few practice two handed imaginary whallops, the heavy pounder stopping short of whomping holes in the ground. When he was ready, he stepped on the platform, swung the thing with the might of a guy whose life was in jeopardy, and watched the clanger rise above him, striking the bell. He turned proudly back to look at the two overwhelmed buddies, both still shocked at the outcome. "There. Beat that, boys." The attendant handed him his prize, a fat cigar.

Henry's success did not sit well with Paul. "Well, geez, Henry. If you can do it, so can I. You've never beat your big brother at anything." Of course Henry had beat him at lots of things, but Paul had selective memory.

Paul took the post maul from Henry's outstretched hands, and proceeded to line himself up, in a similar way Henry had. As Henry was successful, so too should he be. He lifted the sledge far above his head, and brought it down with as much force as he could muster, but missed the circular mark indicating where to hit. The clanger failed to move upwards at all. "Damn. I missed it. I would have hit it hard enough, too."

So he paid the man another quarter, and realigned himself, to try again. The second attempt was better, at least, than the first, but still the clanger only rocketed about three fourths of the way up the pole. Paul watched the upward movement, but could not believe it, when the clanger returned to the ground. "I let up on how hard I swung, so I wouldn't miss the circle again. You must have hit it just in the right spot, Henry," he said, as he paid another quarter for try number three. "This time I'm gonna swing hard, and accurate."

Try number three was only slightly better than try number two, but still there was a long way to go to attain success. Paul looked angrier as he tried for the fourth time, and even angrier on the fifth. "You were just lucky. I bet you couldn't do it again," he dared.

The caretaker of the event stepped in, informing them more formally, "We usually only allow a person to get one cigar at a time. Otherwise someone might come along and clean me out."

"But my brother here was just lucky. Just let him go again. Don't even give him a cigar, if you don't want to. I'll pay for his try, and it'll be fun to see him not make it." Paul convinced the man, who didn't need to be convinced. Competition amongst friends was what made his racket a successful one.

Henry tool the maul from his brother, strode up confidently, took aim, and swung another mighty blow to the red rubbery marker below. To Paul's dismay, the bell on top rang again, even louder than it had the first time. "There," gleamed Henry, "it's easy."

Now Paul was even more disturbed. So much that he took his shirt off, to give himself more freedom of movement. Try number six. "Damn!" Try seven. "Damn." Try eight. "You're an ass, Henry. It's that darn hat. It's brought me bad luck." Try nine. "Next time we'll leave you at your farmer friends." Try ten. "That guy's pushing some button that makes it tougher for me."

The attendant carnie made sure he was standing away from any gadgets for try eleven.

But alas, it was all to no avail. He just wasn't strong enough, or accurate enough. He didn't give up until he had to; the money well in Henry's pocket dried out, exhausted, before even the remnants of Paul's energy.

"Well, that does it, guys. At least I gave it my best shot, didn't I, Denys?" Paul begged his friend for support, in the his idiot behaviour of showing little brother who can do better.

"Yes, Paul, you sure did," replied Denys. Neither he nor Henry wanted to make the situation any worse by reminding him that the money was gone.

"So what do you two want to do now?" asked Paul. "It's too darn bad that Henry bought that stupid hat, or we'd still have lots of money."

Henry and Denys couldn't tell whether he was kidding, or actually mad at Henry, so shut up, hoping another distraction would come along.

The threesome wandered aimlessly about the midway, watching, but not participating, for another hour or so. The only thing that bonded them was the hat, which kept on getting passed around. At least this was theirs to keep, a real item, not just some temporary experience. It provided something to do while they watched others enjoying themselves.

After an hour or so, the threesome headed back up town, having decided to beg on the streets outside the bar for some spare change for food. "Spare change, mister?" said Denys, as a gentleman passed by.

"Sorry, not today." came the polite reply.

Five more polite refusals in a row had the threesome discouraged, so Paul, without discussing it with his companions, tried a new strategy. "Hey, Mister, wanna buy a hat? Two bucks. It's almost new." he asked of the first hatless stranger to wander by.

"No way!" yelled Henry, when the poor fellow, thinking he might just get a deal, stopped to discuss it. Henry wasn't about to give that hat away so easily.

"Maybe if we put the hat, on the ground, and we act like clowns, or sing a song, somebody will be more generous," suggested Denys.

"Clowns we are for sure, but I can't sing, and neither can you guys." Henry wished to keep some dignity. After all, it was only another day, or less, to go.

Soon, as begging was completely unsuccessful, they got back in the car, and drove around without purpose, taking turns wearing the hat, and yelling "Whoopee!" or "Hi, Honey!" to strangers walking about. No point letting others know that they didn't understand how to have fun on such a celebration.

After about an hour of this, Denys looked at the gas gauge, "You know, Paul, if we drive around all night, we'll run out of gas. We'd better stop somewhere." Paul pulled off the street to a park near the downtown part of Wainwright, and the trio strolled through the trees, then along Main Street, begging once or twice, but again with no success. Paul kept reminding his brother of the stupidity of purchasing a cowboy hat, and of how lucky Henry had been at the ringing of the bell. Henry ignored it mostly, and Denys watched, childhood experience having taught him not to take sides in brotherly disputes.

Starving, hopelessly bored, and completely broke, the trio eventually grew restless. By midnight they'd had enough of the situation, and headed north towards Henry's workplace.

"Can we sleep at your place, Henry?" Denys asked.

Henry spoke as though he'd had it prepared, "No way. I told Burns I was gone for the night. Told him we'd be in a hotel. He's told me lots of times not to bring my friends to his place. I guess we'll have to just stay in the car overnight."

Paul pulled the Chevy off onto a gravel road beside the Battle, and parked. "This looks like a good spot. There's water, and it's quiet." Taking turns wearing the hat, the trio eventually all dozed off, but not without standard expected interruptions from wiggling, snoring, hat thieves, into the bushes washroom breaks, and howling coyotes.

Dawn arrived, and Henry announced, sounding relieved that an ordeal had passed, "Now I can go back to Burns' place, and you guys can go home. Gotta work tomorrow, you know."

At Henry's insistence, the trio walked down to the river, and splashed some water on their faces, not wishing to appear that they had spent the night in a car. The cool refreshing water was a decent wake-up, even if none of the bedraggled crew had had a powerful sleep.

When they arrived at Burns' place, Henry decided he should introduce his buddies to his employer. After introductions, Burns invited all three to come on down to the river, something they could do, to pass the time, just to take a look, and perhaps cast in a line. "Nice hat," he complimented Henry, who for the moment had the beauty on.

"I guess we don't need to be home until tonight, so yeah, we might as well come with you." Paul accepted the invitation an behalf of his group.

Without letting Burns and the youngsters who tagged along know that they were already familiar with the bridge spot, Paul and Henry pulled the car back into the same spot they had vacated only half an hour ago. Energetic Burns kids piled out of the half ton, while a contrasting tired threesome of Metis crawled out of their beater.

The entire group proceeded to the middle of the bridge to watch the river below, and to toss rocks, or just aim spit drops on passing bubbles.

"Well, did you guys have a decent time at the rodeo?" Burns inquired, seriously, and wishing to find out more of Henry's friends.

"Oh, yeah, we had a real great time," Henry lied. "We were cowboys, hats and all."

"Betcha that stupid hat won't float past that corner," said Paul, looking downstream a few hundred metres, to where the river bent.

"Sure it will, it's a good hat. It fits Denys there real well. Besides, I paid seven bucks for it, so it has to float." Henry spoke as though he'd seen a hat float before.

"No way," argued Paul, "it'll sink before it gets out of sight."

Without hesitation, and having figured out the immediate solution to the impending argument, Denys took the hat off his own head, and backflung it off the bridge, out over the water. "We'll see who's right this time," he informed them, as the hat floated beautifully in the air, and slowly settled down to the water.

The Burns kids looked on in dismay, not at all realizing the significance of the moment, at the sight of this almost brand new expensive looking hat so carefree floating along, slowly losing ground to the river water, and eventually disappearing from sight, having breathed it's last Stetson breath, having caused it's last argument, and carrying with it not so good memories of a sojourn into cowboyhood. To the collection of naive farmer children, the Metis threesome seemed oddly detached, even relieved, a puzzling situation for the onlookers. Not something Dad would have done.

"Well, I guess Paul is right this time," Henry laughed. "You win, Paul." He stuck out his hand to congratulate his brother's good fortune at winning, this time, a gentleman's bet, as no money had been gambled.

Then he turned to Burns. "Do you think my brother here could have five bucks worth of gas. I'll pay you by working for free tomorrow."

"Sure, Henry. No problem," smiled Burns.

# Ol’ One Eye

Ol’ One-Eye, as he came to be known, was the darndest fish. No other fish, at least not that any of the oldtime fishermen of the Battle knew, had ever attained such legendary status as this fellow had. No fish, before or after, had been captured as many times as he, nor so many hooks lost, nor fishermen frustrated.

His sojourn into war with humankind began back in about July of 1960, when a fella named Tony Hansen, a pig farmer, first caught him. At that time he was just a wee fish, more of a minnow, and hadn’t even really been caught at all, but had fallen into the misfortune of being snagged by Tony, on one of those monstrous large red and white spoons.

“Darn fish was smaller than the stupid spoon,” Tony had explained. “I can’t believe that he was close to the hook at all. In fact he was probably running from it. Probably thought that it was a larger pike, and was after him. Anyways, the hook was embedded in his eye, and when we tried to dislodge it, the hook pulled the thing’s eye right out. He wasn’t worth keeping at all, so I just threw him back in, and I never figured that he’d live.”

But the sucker must have, because later that fall, Tony’s cousin, a monster man, also a bacon rancher, named Shorty, was trying his luck at the same rapids, when he too snagged a fish, this time by the tail. Only later did the two of them get to figurin’ it was the same fish. “Weirdest thing, Tony,” said Shorty, “I caught this fish that only had one eye. It just had an empty socket on the other side. Kind of ugly, really, and it sure wasn’t worth keeping, so I tossed the poor creature back in.”

Tony reflected, “You know, Shorty, maybe that was the same darn fish I caught at that hole in July. I threw one back in, that I had snagged the eye of.”

“Could be,” replied Shorty. “Don’t matter much now anyway. So we both caught a tiny jack that we threw back in. Big deal.”

Ol’ One-Eye must have figured it was a pretty big deal, all right, as his untimely death had been avoided twice, in that same summer, and in similar ways, that of being snagged, and thrown back in. Just a good thing for him he was still so small.

But these fish have the ways of nature about them. Fish grow, you know, and the next summer, Tony was back at his favorite hole. So was Ol’ One-Eye. Of course at the time he wasn’t known as Ol’ One’Eye, he was just a stupid little fish with one eye, like the runt of the litter, just managing somehow eek out a survival on the trash that floated down the rapid.

Somehow, he must have managed to winter in the hole below the rapid, with the flowing water being enough to provide sufficient oxidation. The spring of '61 was the time of his third encounter with hook and line. Tony brought along his son, Jacob, this time, and together the father and son were enjoying the early morning sunshine beside the gurgling rapid. Ol' One-Eye had only grown a bit over the winter, what with foraging on rapid fare being poor. It was young Jacob who caught him, and reeled him close to shore, close enough for Tony to notice the missing eye. Alas, Jacob's inexperience had made the knot of line to leader weak, and a quick turn and tug by One-Eye was all she wrote.

Tony looked curiously at his kid, "You know, son, I think that's the same darn litle fish that your Uncle Shorty and I both caught here last year."

"How come, Dad. Why do ya think that?" asked Jacob.

"Did you see his eye? Looked to me like he had a missing eye on one side."

Jacob didn't believe. "Dad, I think you're seeing things."

Tony had thought about it. "That fish ain't seeing things very well, either, what with only one eye. He probably always has to stay on the same side of the rapid, so he can see things floating by. You know how some fish are bottom feeders, and others are surface feeders? Well I would say this guy is a one sided feeder. What do you think, son?"

Jacob said, "I think you're taking this too far, Dad. You don't even know if it's the same fish, or if he had one eye."

"Well, I reckon if I'm right, he'll be healed in a month or so, and we'll just have to come back and check it out," Tont vowed.

Meanwhile, spring had sprung, and so did vegetation, and with it minnows, and other edible creatures. One-Eye was just about last on the food chain around here except for man, and bigger pike, so the pickings along the running water improved, allowing One-Eye to gain both weight, and strength.

Jacob and Tony got to talking fishing with Uncle Shorty one day, and One-Eye came up. "You know, Shorty, I think I caught that same fish again. Jacob and me were down there at the rapid, and Jacob had one on, but he got away. Still a little fish, but when I went over to help land it, I'm pretty darned sure the thing had only one eye. Do you remember which side it was on?"

Shorty didn't really care. "Doesn't really matter, does it? What do you think, Jacob? Is Dad just pulling one over on you?"

"Yes, Uncle, that's what I think," Jacob stated his opinion clearly.

"Well, I don't know about your dad, but I sure wouldn't try to pull your leg. I caught a one-eyed fish last fall. Could be the same fish, all right." Shorty turned to his brother. "How come you care which eye it was?"

Tony explained. "Well, I was just figurin' that it would always be on the same side of the rapid is all. If you wanted to catch that same fish, you'd have a better chance of catching it on one side or the other cause it only can see one way."

But Shorty, figuring to be smarter, had a better idea. "You don't have to figure that out, you know. If we can all remember where we hooked it, that'll help. I remember where I hooked it. It was just this side of the flowing water, about three metres past where the back eddy starts."

Tony was getting really intrigued now. He'd always wondered how many times the same fish could get away from different fishermen, but this was better, because you knew for sure or almost for sure, if it *was* the same fish or not, unless of course there were two one-eyed fish, which was highly unlikely. "That's where I caught it too, or thereabouts, anyway. What about you, Jake?"

Jake answered, still disbelieving, "Well, that is where I caught the fish all right, but I don't think this proves anything. Until we actually land the thing, we have no proof, and as far as I know, you two could be making this whole thing up just to hassle me."

"Us, Jake?" replied Shorty. "Nah. Tell you what. Let's give it about a month, and we'll all go togther and try again. How's that sound?"

Jake agreed, "Fine by me."

It wasn't until about August that the trio found the time to return. They drove down with only one intention: to catch One-Eye, and prove or disprove the theory. A warm August evening on the Battle, when there had been no rain for three weeks made the conditions ideal. But alas, it was not to be. Skunked, rained-out, zippo. All the fish were either not hungry, or not there at all. It was disappointing, as much hype about the stupid one-eyed fish had gone on ever since they'd discussed it.

Jacob was the least upset, as somehow this laid credence to his theory, at least. "I told you guys the thing didn't exist. It was just a silly story, you guys made up."

Uncle Shorty wasn't so quick to give up. "You know, Jake, just because we didn't catch him doesn't mean he ain't here, now does it. Perhaps he's just right out there in the water, but just ain't hungry."

Jake contemplated, "I suppose, but I still don't think so, Uncle."

Shorty said, "Well, I for one, am not giving up. I'm going to come back. If I catch him, I'll be over to show you."

"Sure, Uncle. I'll admit I'm wrong when you do that. But for now I'm right, I guess, eh? It's just another 'The One That Got Away' story."

Over the next few years, Tony and Jacob, or Shorty by himself, or sometimes all three would return to the same rapid, looking for Ol' One-Eye, as the phantom fish was called. Although they caught lots of walleye, goldeye, and other pike, rarely getting skunked, One-Eye was never hooked again. They succumbed to the reality that this would be just another barely believable tale for the grandchildren some day.

However, upon the Battle, there were other holes, and other fishermen, and these guys talked, over coffee, at the community picnics, and just about whenever they got together. The fishermen, who were few and far between, even amongst the locals, usually talked fishing. It wasn't until the summer of '68, seven years later, that a one-eyed fish became a topic of anyone's conversation.

A fellow named Byron, but nicknamed Barny, who lived about ten miles west of Shorty on the north side of the Battle, known to cast a few lines into the water on the occasional warm summer evening, started it all. He was talking to Shorty at a ball game, and in a lull in the usual topic, that of the market price of pork, he just asked, "Done any fishing in the river lately, Shorty?"

"No," answered Shorty, "A few years back they used to bite. I guess I've been down only once in the last couple of years. Why?"

Byron retold his story. "Well, I was down there the other night, you know, right by the Kinsley bridge, and the weirdest thing happened. I hooked something, I'm pretty sure it was a walleye, but I got it right up close to shore, and this monster of a pike came right up after it, and took it right off the hook. The weird thing wasn't the pike taking the walleye. That's happened to me before. But the weird thing was that it seemed that the stupid pike only had one eye. I mean, I got a pretty good look at it, and all. It was a long one, for the Battle anyway. Musta been six pounds or so. Not many people believe me, and I thought you might, since I know you go down sometimes."

Shorty's face perked up. "Well, you know, we did think there was a one-eyed fish down there. Tony threw one back after the hook pulled it's eye out, and I threw a little one-eyed one back the same year. Then the next spring young Jake almost landed one that Tony saw, and thought it only had one eye. We tried in the same spot for a few times after that, but we never caught it. I suppose it could be the same fish. Where'd you catch it, again?"

Barny, too, was now more alert in the conversation. "Just below the bridge, you know, there's sort of an island and some rapids."

Shorty continued, "Well, the one we caught was about a mile downstream from there. I suppose it could be the same fish. Maybe he just moved upstream a little on us. We even had a name for him."

"What?" inquired Barny.

"Ol One-Eye, of course," said Shorty, shrugging as though Barny should have known.

"I should have guessed. You never know. Not many one-eyed fish in there."

"What side of the river were you on?" asked Shorty, wanting to get the story exact.

"The south. Why?"

Shorty explained his theory. "Well, back then I figured he'd always be on the same side of the river every time, since he only has one eye, he'd have to watch from the same side all the time."

Barny thought it made sense. "Yeah, I suppose that figures."

Shorty couldn't wait to tell Jacob and Tony of the news, so the next morning he drove over to their place, and greeted them with, "Guess what?"

"What, Uncle?" asked Jake, who was now 14.

"I was talking to old Barny last night at the ball game at Pallsburg Hall, and it seems he saw a one-eyed fish down by the bridge. You guys remember a few years back, eh?"

Jake was intrigued. "Yeah, I remember we argued whether the thing even existed, and as I recall we agreed that I was right, unless you caught it, and proved me wrong."

Shorty enthusiastically informed them. "Well, I'm gonna go down to the bridge tonight and do just that. You want to come along?"

Jake liked the idea. "Sure. Might as well. Haven't been down there for awhile anyway. I don't mind if you prove yourself wrong again."

"Jake, you can never disprove almost any fishing story, unless it's extremely exaggerated."

"Yeah, I suppose, but this one's a bit wild," said Jake.

His uncle wanted so badly to convince Jake of the possibility. "I know Barny pretty good. He's not one to BS much."

"Uncle, when you get it mounted on the wall, you can brag all you want."

That evening, about seven, after supper, and allowing for a couple of hours before darkness, the optimist picked up the pessimist, and away the half ton rumbled, down to the bridge.

After a few fishless casts, Jake gave his uncle a dig, "Well, obviously, One-Eye ain't here. Neither are any others. Do you want to go home yet?"

"No, just because he isn't where Barny saw him doesn't mean he isn't close by somewhere. Maybe he moved back to the other rapid where we first caught him. We still have time. Let's go down there."

"Okay," agreed Jake. "You're the driver. I got nothing better to do."

At the rapid, Jake, being more prepared than his uncle, hurried to get to the best spot, and cast out. Right away he yelled, "Hey, Uncle, guess what? I think I got one."

Shorty, actually surprised, tried to sound like he wasn't. "Well, what do you know, kid. Barny was right. There are fish in here. I'll be right over to help you land him."

Jake knew what his uncle was thinking. "So you think it's One-Eye. Such a fool. It's pulling pretty hard, though."

Shorty advised, "Well, you take it real easy now. Don't lose him. Work him over slow."

"I know what I'm doing, Uncle."

"That's what they all say."

Jake, now excited, spoke louder, "Whoa. He *is* a big one. It's a pickerel, though. I can see. Too bad. It's not ol' One-Eye, but we better land him anyway. I can see the hook. It's barely even in his mouth."

"You be careful," Shorty cautioned, not wishing it to end in a getaway. "A big pickerel is better than a one-eyed pike any day. A lot better eating."

"Uncle, I think there's something following it, too. Looks like a jack. A real big jack."

Shorty supposed, "That's One-Eye, I bet."

"I don't know. I'm just going to land the walleye. We'll get the pike later." Jake was getting the walleye close to the rocks beneath his feet. He could see both fish clearly now. It seemed that if he brought the walleye in real smooth, without any fighting, the pike would follow. He had to be still, though. Meanwhile, Uncle Shorty had arrived on the scene. "Move slowly, Uncle. They're both real close."

Uncle was whispering now, "Wow, look at that. Tell you what. You try the walleye. I'm going after the pike. Hold it still. Don't even crank any more til I get out there."

"Okay, uncle. You tell me when you're ready." Shorty peered into the water to get a better look at the pike. Sure enough. It only had one eye. That's why it was probably acting so stupidly. He got himself to the side that had no eye, and within pouncing distance.

"Okay, son, I'm ready," he whispered. "Try your best to land it." Just as Jake started bending forward to grab the leader, the walleye spooked, and leapt clear out of the water, in a valiant attempt to get away.

Shorty dove, his huge belly making a horrendous splash, and his arms stretched out to grab the pike, with those muscular farmer hands of his. He managed to grasp hold of the creature on both sides, just behind the gills, and then he just rolled over onto the rocks, with the mighty slough shark flailing away with all it's body, right above him. He hung on, like a running back hangs on to a football when he hits the line. His experience in greased hog competitions at the country fairs of childhood came in handy, with the slippery fish.

Jake, in the meantime, managed to grab the leader of the walleye, and lift it up out of the water, but it too, with a quick strong flip, spat out the hook, and headed in a beeline back to deeper water. However, it encountered this virtual dam in the name of Shorty, and was stranded in shallower water, with no obvious escape route. "Stay down, Uncle, you've got the walleye stranded. It's got nowhere to go."

"But I want to keep ol' One-Eye here." The pike was twisting and turning with all it's might, but somehow Shorty hung on.

Eventually, although his hands got cut by the walleye's sharp fin, Jake got hold of both sides, and was able to toss it about five metres out of the water, using both hands, and all his might. "One down. One to go. What do you want me to do?"

"Well, it's going to be hard for me to get up, and not lose the fish." Jake could not risk trying to take the fish from Uncle, yet Uncle had neither hand free, so could not roll over to push himself up. The only thing poor Jake could do was to get sort of under his uncle's rear end and shove to help get the old boy up on his feet. With a mighty heave ho from Jake, and a simultaneous fling from Uncle as he rose, the pike came to rest along side it's prey, the walleye.

"Well, what do you know, Jake, would you look at that!" Shorty was overwhelmed.

Jake already had plans. "I think, Uncle, we should get the pair of them mounted by that taxidermist in town."

"For sure," agreed Shorty. "Absolutely!"

Which is, of course, what they did. Then whenever a fish story telling competition came along, the pair could have proof of their tale. To this day, even though poor old Shorty has passed on, Jake at least has proof, on his wall, if a fellow doesn't believe. It's engraved, "Ol' One-Eye and His Walleye Friend - Battle River, Summer, 1968."

Now that's the truth.

# Crossing

Battle is a snaky mellow charmer of a femme, usually. But hidden beneath her tranquil surface are two devils. One is Current, the other is Depth. Each is a hideous being on its own, and tornado like in ability to surprise. They often work their evilness together, with Current being the alluring trap, and Depth being the finisher, coming in for the kill, only after friend Current had done His evil set up deed. Tools of the Great Equalizer's trade include hidden rocks or logs, the ability of Current to hide, seasonal shifting of sand, and the beckoning call of 'the other side' allowing Current and Depth to serve their master well, enabling Him to feast at least once or twice a year.

Man has warned himself of the two demons lurking there, by posting no uncertain terms signage such as "SWIM AT YOUR OWN RISK" or "BEWARE OF CURRENT", wherever humans might entertain the thought of refreshing dips. At a few spots, humankind has gone so far to erect a fence or two. To intelligent man's dismay, the non readers of signs, the young bravado drunken ones, the naive children not yet trained in arts of swimmage, or the plain foolhardy, have entertained themselves despite the heeds, and suffered a water filled lung at the hands of either of the two devils, or both.

Other rivers are less deceptive settings, where Current and Depth have less opportunity for disguise. Battle is a more willing place, being that it is so weak and trusting in appearance, so much so, that man pretends, or even scoffs at the suggestion of the Devils hiding here, "You're kidding. That place is no deeper than my butt. No one could possibly drown there." Another potential victim takes the bait, entering the foray of unsuspecting naivety, like too many fools before him.

Man derives joy at tempting the oh so ready demon pair, and more often than not pulls a fellow man out at only the last opportunity available. For every drowning, there are twenty near drownings, as for every car fender bender, there are twenty "That was close!"s.

The Battle had a curve there, and an obvious deep hole beside the curve. But the sand on the other side was a beach. This side was a slimehole, rocky, and unfit for beachhood at all. The appealing sand across there enticed the threesome, magnetic. "Come over here. Build me, change me. I am yours today."

To cross was an easy matter. Seventy or eighty metres upstream from the beach was an easy crossing place, shallow enough to wade, and only gravel on the bottom, not those nasty rocks which could twist ankles, and cut feet, hence disabling the crosser. Danny, aged twelve, a swimmer, was the first to go, the pioneer, the scout. The others watched for his success. After less than a minute, and as he was going up the other side, he called back, "It's easy. There are no rocks. It's not deep at all." His words held truth as the crossing had been quick, and the water had hardly entertained his belly button.

Brother Bob, aged ten, he too a swimmer, if only for a year, was next in line, his confidence boosted by Danny the elder. He too, attempted the same feat, tempting his fate if only a little, and secured the crossing in only ten seconds longer than Danny had, water arriving only at his solar plexus.

Cousin Darlene, only ten, and shorter yet than Bob called out, "I'm scared."

"It's nothing, Darlene. Didn't you watch us?" Danny called back, as he and brother headed for the sandy beach, and safety, castles just waiting to manifest from his creative hands.

Bob, too, added, "If I can make it, so can you. Besides, you can swim better than I, can't you?" knowing she had two years of lessons over his one. He sped ahead to catch the leader, as always.

A moment of decision had arrived for Darlene. She had come here to experience life, with these guys, as they had predicted she would, and to have loads of mind expanding fun. So far they had lived up to last winter's Christmas promise of two weeks of adventurous outings on the farm. Today was day three of her time with the cousins, which to date had been a marvelous break from the city, and it's lack of nature. Today's sojourn involved the threesome riding bicycles to the river, where the boycousins had promised to share their knowledge of water, and sand.

Now, here she sat, perplexed and over here, on this dirty grass, and there they were, two fun-loving creative cousins, on the other side, where entertainment for the afternoon was just starting. The choices were obvious. Stay here and mope all afternoon, or get out of chickenhood, and cross this unfamiliar river, and join in the fun. It was only one o'clock. Four hours of moping seemed eternal. Being younger, and perhaps just a tagalong, meant they probably wouldn't be back, for at least an hour.

She went for it, facing the fear head on. As she stepped in, it felt cold, but soon her feet adjusted to the temperature, and she mosied further. She could not remember exactly where they had entered and exited, and she could still see the cousin's backsides, although they were becoming less visible with each second of her hesitation. She realized she'd better hurry if they were to not get out of sight, or worse, out of calling range. She quickened the pace, and changed her angle unknowingly, more in their direction, as her head turned to watch them disappear from sight.

By now she was up to her waist, and the bottom seemed not to be getting even, but still deepening. She tried to remember her height as compared to

Bob's but could not. She guessed they were similar. She glanced down to see the remnants of her navel disappear. "My face must look awful," she thought, "too bad there's no one here to see it. If cousins were still here, they'd help, I could yell at them."

She now felt the current stronger from the greater submersion, and had to lean into it a bit, like leaning into wind. Her leading toe bumped into something hard. "A rock, or log," she thought. She moved her toes, and felt the six inch high boulder, and it's flat algae covered top. She reasoned that if she stood on it, she could sort of dive, and swim straight ahead, easily achieving her predetermined goal, the sacred other side. "For sure, I'm crossing back with Danny," she thought ahead four hours.

She got one foot up on the rock, and paused in prayer, before shifting her weight to it. Prayer lost, the final shift of weight did her in. As she lifted the trailing foot, the front one gave out to the slippery algae, and over she went, captured by Current, the demon. She panicked, went under, and forgot everything she had ever learned about anything. Her arms began flailing, and she screamed, "DANNY, HELP ME!" She was able to grab one more breath, and scream another shortened version of "HELP ME!" before Current did his hungry ugly deed of pulling her legs farther under. The demon had tasted her now.

Screams were to no avail. Danny was entertained, around the corner, marking out a perfect square in the sand, where he was about to construct the most awesome sand castle, ever. He and Bob were chattering away competitively about Danny's proposal, an afternoon castle contest. "I can build a better one than you can," he informed his brother.

Bob accepted the invitation, as usual, but not wholeheartedly, and forced his voice to sound challenged. "We'll see about that."

"Tell you what. Darlene can be the judge," Danny suggested.

"I suppose that's okay. She likes you better than me, though. Hopefully she can be fair." Bob did not like any of the advantages that his brother could dream up. He usually lost at these building, thinking, or athletic competitions, even without the older brother's aid of having a biased judge. He harboured an ongoing resentment which seemed to loom larger each day, an unavoidable lifetime situation of self esteem destruction. This time he was resigned to participation, for being called a chicken in front of the cousin would be even worse than losing.

"I don't see any other way we can do it. If you and I vote, it'll be a tie." Danny liked this. Anything to out do his sucker brother, and impress the cousin. He revelled in watching Bob become mush. All the better with a witness.

"Yeah, I guess so." Bob was resigned. He would give his darndest anyway, even if he had to face another round of the ego inspired disdain his brother would dish out. At least it was something to do. And perhaps, just a slim perhaps, Darlene would like his better.

Bob stood to marvel his own initial castle plan, scratched in sand, a not so circular circle. “By the way, Danny, where is Darlene? She should be here pretty soon, shouldn’t she?”

At this Danny stood up from his just begun masterpiece, realizing that Bob, the idiot, for once was right, and started to walk back along the curved sandy shore. Within half a minute, from a crested dune, he spotted a still struggling head, bobbing along the current, well out over his head, in the middle of the stream. She was obviously in trouble. He called back, “Bob, get over here!”

Bob recognized the voice’s urgency, and came running. By the time he arrived, Danny was well out into the water, at a position where he figured he could grab her as she floated by, with minimal swimming effort or danger, on his part. It was getting deeper than he figured, so he turned and yelled back, panic in his voice, “Go get a long tree, or stick, or something you can help with,” and dove in, using whatever his twelve year old upper body strength had in it.

Swimming hard, he arrived at the bobbing head, and realized he could no longer touch bottom. Not being a really strong swimmer, and untrained, he made a quick decision to go down with her, if necessary. He managed to grab one of her arms with his, and struggled to pull her towards shore. His objective was just to get her out first, not to have her breathe out there. He could do life saving resuscitation later. There was no grip along the bottom, and her legs kept bumping into his, as he tried unsuccessfully to kick for shore. Together the pair bobbed along, with only he surfacing for irregular gasps of vital air. He wished he could yell at her to calm down, but her frenzy outweighed the possibility of that having any success.

Soon his wishes and fears coincided, as she started struggling less, and less. He was unsure whether it was his hand, in comfort, or if she was dying on him, right out there. He reasoned, that if her becoming still was comfort, then oxygen filled lungs must be comforting. Dreadfully, he realized the truth of her condition.

Meanwhile, Bob had managed to secure a dead tree, only about eight feet long, but it would have to do. There was no time for searching out a better one. He too, judged the current, ran downstream, and strode in, hands above, and shoving the tree along the water’s surface, narrow end first, out ahead of himself, and downstream from the struggling twosome.. He called, “Danny, grab the tree!”

Danny managed to reach out with his free hand and grip it, one handed, right at the very end. Bob was chest deep into the water, and had very poor traction, half floating with current, but enough at least to slow the flow a bit. Either he would join them, becoming a floating three, or Current would lose. Slowly he coerced the pair closer to shore. Eventually, the traction became better, the water shallower, and he released his grip on the pole, moving over to help Danny haul the now still cousin to shore, mind racing with dreadful horrid outcomes.

Danny remembered somewhat vaguely, the swimming lesson part on mouth to mouth, even if it was his first, hopefully last, time for applied knowledge, and administered the aid to his cousin, while Bob pleadingly rubbed her feet, as if to massage lifeforce back into her from there. After a few solid full lunged breaths of air from Danny, the would-be corpse sputtered, an engine gurgling to start. Slimy colored water gushed out of her mouth, as Danny turned her head to face the gentle sandy slope, the regurgitated muck trickling down to the river's edge. Current and Depth had been foiled this time. They waited patiently, a few metres away, knowing some other victim would appear some day for their relentless appetites.

Darlene came to, amidst the sputtering and vomiting of river water. Her eyes opened, and she slowly recuperated from the ordeal, eventually able to sit up, and consciously sense the scary situation that had just occurred.

"You okay?" Danny asked.

"Uh, yeah, I guess so." she managed a half smile.

"That's good." Danny's face showed relief, big time.

"Yes." The half smile transformed into a full blown one, as she shook her head, still in shock, "Thanks, guys."

Bob looked at her now rekindled eyes, "You really had us scared, Darlene. Boy, it was close. You could easily have been a gonner. Danny, too, maybe." In the afterthought, Bob felt that Danny could have been swallowed with her, leaving him, the younger brother, to relay the message by bike or panicked running to the unknowing parents up the hill above the valley some three long miles away. He shuddered at the thought.

She glowingly returned Bob's stare. "Well, guys, it's okay now. In a while, I'm sure I'll feel better. Right now I feel like throwing up some more." She improved by the second, wiggled her feet, moved her arms, and tried to stand, only to be blocked by Danny's caring arm.

He said, calmly now, "Sit for a while longer. Don't stand until you feel very ready. We have all day. From what I know of this, you're right, you will improve. You'll feel a little wobbly for a while is all, and you probably won't be able to do a lot of work. I guess you'll have to watch us build a sand castle. Danny and I will build one just for you. The two of us were planning one all along. Right, Bob."

Bob agreed, "Right, Danny," as he shuffled over to rid the sand of his not so perfect circle.

# R. T. McGee - The Cow

A hermit's life without a car involves hitchhiking. R.T., known as Ronny, to friends, had to use his thumb, once a month, to get to town. Some obliging passer-by always picked him up, and dropped him off. All he had to do was walk to his gate, and wait. Within an hour, some willing driver would happen along. A few hours in town, a mile walk back to the road, stick out the thumb again, and Ronny would have a successful supply getting day.

The building of the new straight highway changed all that. The traffic switched from 100 passers-by a day, to maybe two, on a good day. So Ronny had to settle with the neighbour to the north, and get some commitment from him to stop by, on a regular basis. Pete Marvin was his man. Pete lived to the north, already was a partner in sharecropping of greenfeed, and the old highway was Pete's cut off anyway, so checking on Ronny wasn't a problem.

"Do you think you could stop by on a regular basis, Pete?" Ronny had asked, about three months after the highway opened, and he realized the lack of significant traffic was a problem.

"Give me a little money for gas once in a while, and sure, I'll do it. Not a problem at all." Pete kind of liked the old hermit, anyway. Ronny always had stories to share, or certainly personality quirks to observe. Bringing him to town was the neighbourly thing to do, and usually every Friday, Pete made the trip, either with a load of grain, or to get his own supplies.

Ronny had purchased two quarters of land at a decent price, along a long draw that meandered for about five miles into the Battle. A scenic spot, along the narrow, winding road, as early surveyors had used the draw as a means of gaining a slowly elevating path, back when road building equipment consisted of horse drawn graders, and no real earth movement could occur. It meant for some extremely sharp corners, barely negotiable by grain trucks, and not negotiable by the new trailer trucks at all. Hence the new highway. There were thirty broke fenced acres up on the flats above, where Ronny had recently negotiated with Pete, to have Pete plant greenfeed, to keep the few cattle alive during the harsh Alberta winters. Not a bad setup.

R.T. McGee hadn't bothered to fence in his house from the cattle, but had just located it on a hillside, in the middle of the pasture land where the cattle roamed. A few hundred yards up the steep hill was where the greenfeed field was, and he could walk up there to access the wooden half-a-corral and chute, where the cattle wintered, and were loaded for market. Selection of the house site, in the beginning, had been done exactly for this purpose. Halfway between the road, and the cultivated field, where the two walks he needed to take would be easily managed. He built a two room log hut, more or less, one room for sleeping, and the other for cooking, and sitting. When electricity, and telephones came along, Ronny declined on getting connected up, as there was no useful purpose to it. With the help of neighbours like Pete, who needs all that extra crap around? Just he, and his cattle. The draw held a spring for water, and the road across it to his place formed a natural looking dam, which held back water in a small deep, but totally functional slough-reservoir. It was far more efficient to have a neighbour help him round up a few of the bovine, and take them off to market, in town, than it was to buy your own truck. Vehicles frightened him. Noisy contraptions, always breaking down. More waste of valuable time.

Living right on the pasture catalysed oddness in his cattle. Mainly, it tamed them. He fit right in on their landscape, like an old rundown no longer in use shed or granary would. To the cows, his place was nothing more than a big square flat tree. His slow movements and friendly manner amidst them calmed them. Their proximity to him aided his ability to control them, as he named them all, and talked to them, as if they were his human companions. A deep but soft voice soothed their natures whenever they were giving birth to calves, or fighting over who should get the best spot on the greenfeed line. In winter, when snow was far too deep for natural grasses, they learned to watch for him, waiting hungrily by his house, for him to come out, and proceed up the hill, where the meal, and dessert lay. Greenfeed. He played pied piper to them, using their worn cow trail, a winding foot wide path beaten down through the snow in winter, and sod in summer, up the hill. His downhill trek was lonely, as they stayed up to re chew on the feed. Cattle can chew cuds forever, a lot worse than kids with favorite gum. The cattle seemed to worship him, as gentle provider he was. Without him, they would die a cold starving death.

One night, the third Saturday in February, it was forty below, and the wind was howling around the shack, the cows all around it, seeking shelter from the wind, and the bit of warmth that Ronny's wood stove provided through the uninsulated structure. Inside, he slept restlessly, although his many blankets warmed him, his beloved cattle seemed uneasy. "Poor beasts," he thought, "must be damn hard on them tonight."

It was only a few days before the real brunt of calving season, so about two a.m., he decided to go for a stroll, and have a look-see, just in case one of the poor things was calving. He already had two calves on his hands, but they were each a few days old, and had hardened up to the weather. He lit his coal oil lamp and set out. The group was huddled on the south side of his shack, out of the wind, as much as possible, in circular fashion. Some had bedded down, while others remained standing, gently mooing about one of his tamed beauts, Elly. She was down, and when he approached her behind, sure enough, as he had feared, she was in the beginning calving stages, and obviously in trouble.

"That damn new bull," he thought to himself. "She's never had trouble before. Must have a big calf in there." He slapped a few behinds to move the other compassionate cattle out of the way, set his lantern down in the straw, and approached Elly's neck, and head, figuring the least he could do was move her over to right beside his shack, where she'd be warmer. The two cows with calves had chosen that spot, or had been given it by the others, so he had to swat them to get them out of the way to make room for Elly, in her distress. This was not what he wanted to be doing in forty below weather, but what the heck, she was a cow, his bovine friend, and losing her, or her calf would be a monetary setback. Not that he couldn't handle that, it was the principle of not having cows dying on you that had him so attached to the freezing ordeal. She was the patient, and he the doctor, and the hospital was damn cold.

With some pulling, and gentle persuasion, "C'mon, Old Girl, I just have to move you a few yards," he succeeded in getting her to move.

She stood, her deep soft eyes staring at the old guy, in bovine love for her owner, and murmuring away in cowtalk, "Just what the heck are you trying to do to me? Whatever it is, I hope it helps, cause I sure don't feel very good right now. I guess you know what's best."

She had been tamed so much by him, that he could lead her just by putting his arm around her neck, and gently walking. He had become their all-loving master, damn near their God. In her situation, desperate as it was, she followed obediently, instinctively, with little persuasion, as any newborn mammal heads for the security of its mother's breast. When he got her close to his shed, he stopped, and tried to push her down onto the recently abandoned, but already warm, spot, of one of her bovine sisters.

She got stubborn with him, deciding to no longer co-operate, an about turn in trust, as though she now felt him to be a softhead veterinarian, not capable of giving any care at all. "What's all this. You got me up just to move me over here. Jeez." It was either stubbornness or she had given up on her situation, too weakened from the pushing ordeal.

Either way, even though he practically climbed on top of her neck to get her to go down, she just wasn't about to. After about five minutes, he reasoned that she'd probably lie down if he just went on inside. Perhaps in half an hour he'd return, and investigate her progress, so having given up on the care, temporarily, he headed around the corner to the shack's door.

When he pulled the handle, and turned back a bit, he realized she had followed him. "You stupid old guy. You thought you could make me lie down there, when you get to go right inside. That's not fair. I'm just going to come right in with you, if you'll allow it."

He realized right away that he had a dilemma on his hands. Obviously, she wanted to follow him in, to the warmth of his house, about 45 degrees warmer than out there, in the devil's element. This was where she ought to be. He wished he'd bothered to build a barn, but he hadn't, so either she stay out there, and most likely die calving, along with the young fellow, or heifer, inside her, or he let her come in to his cramped living space, where her chances of survival would be at least doubled. For the calf, quadrupled. He let her follow him.

"Thanks, pal, about time you made a correct decision," she mooed.

She, once inside the welcoming space, had to shift to one side just to allow the poor chap enough room to get behind, and shut the door.

"Well, Elly, I guess it's just you and me for the night, eh?" He still had mixed feelings, but now that she was inside, there seemed to be less commotion outside, and there was a strange animal comfort here, despite the smell of bovine permeating the air.

Once he got back around her, she lay down, taking up most of the floor space, but leaving him room to attend to the kitchen area. He moved into the back room, hung up his wretched old parka on the nail, and went back to the kitchen to put some more wood in the stove, and make himself a strong brew of coffee, figuring he might just need it, to keep up through the night. She watched him carefully, but was surely gaining trust of the human's compassion. This was where she belonged, for sure.

The coffee tasted bitter, and hot. He figured he ought to offer his guest some, but knew she'd decline the offer, being as it was so hot. Then the thought struck him that the effects of the brew might just help her along. Certainly it couldn't hurt so he put the remainder of the liquid over by the doorjamb so it would cool down faster from the cold air blowing under the door. He took another look at her behind, but there was no feet showing yet, so he crawled back to his own bed, setting the steady lamp on the cupboard by the stove. He figured he might as well get some sleep, and perhaps he could help her to bear the calf, when she was ready. There was no point in helping a cow until she was darn ready.

In about half an hour, Elly started gently grunting, and making cow birthing sounds, "Get up, you old goat. I need help, and it's your rancher duty to help me," so he hopped up, out of a snoring session.

The first impression Ronny got was her face, which strained from all the work. He poked his way beyond her to the now cooled coffee pot, poured it all into his washbasin, and took it back to her head, pushing it up under her nose to let her know he'd brought her something to drink.

She partook of the brew, and snorted about half of it out through her nostrils onto the floor, as the taste hit. "Yuch! You moron! I'm supposed to be drinking real cold spring water, not this crap."

He reasoned some of it must have gone down, and hoped that it would have at least some stimulant effect for her, although he could never be sure.

Then he moved around to her behind, moved her tail to the side, and saw two wet hooves sticking out, enough already to tie a rope to. This was no time to be idle, so he reached for the lariat beside the outside door, and looped it around the calves hooves, hoping it would stay, and he could help her in the miracle of birth. There was little room in here, barely enough for the big new arrival to land, somewhere, between Ronny, and the door. He needed to sit, behind her, with his old leather mittens on to prevent rope burn, and use her hips to brace his feet, to pull with all his sixty-year old hermit strength.

She pushed, he pulled, in thirty second intervals. The hereford calf's head came, after the hooves, and when the shoulders came, so did the rest of him, a gargantuan bull of a calf, in one final swoosh, sounding like a huge slurp. The calf, all wet, and sticky, fell between Ronny's legs, and Ronny crashed into the door, in a sigh of exhaustion, and relief. Vet-Hermit had come through. The first rays of morning sunshine shone through his window to the south, as he stood, careful not to slip, to admire the miracle.

He moved up to look at Elly's face, and saw that she too, had experienced work, probably a hundred times more than he. Her eyes were half closed, and if she wasn't dying, she was going to sleep. She mooed softly, "I'm tired, Buddy." Ronny looked into the brown eyes, and spoke, "Old Girl, you did fine. Take a break. I'll take care of that young guy for you."

Then he moved to the calf, and began rubbing it down, getting rid of the slime, being the surrogate mother, his hands replacing her tongue. It was the best he could do. Elly certainly wasn't up to it. The young bull's nostrils were a bit plugged with mucus, so he dug in and cleaned as well as he could, eventually deciding to perform mouth to mouth on it, just to be sure. To his wonder and relief, the thing gave a mighty beller, opened it's eyes, and looked right at him, groaning in calf lingo, "Hey, what to heck is that? My instinct tells me this isn't normal."

What a sight to see, too, the old grizzled human, right there, staring back. Poor calf. It tried to stand, and he grabbed it around its torso to help. It wobbled but managed to get erect, and started gawking around for something to drink, "I'm hungry, Mister. Where's that teat?"

With all Ronny's attention focussed on the calf, he had not noticed the fact Elly's breathing had stopped entirely. When his eyes followed the young 'un's, it dawned on the old goat that the poor cow had succumbed. From the labor. From the temperature change. From his coffee. However, in death, reasons don't count, and Ronny had to figure out a plan for his two problems: saving the poor calf, and getting Elly's carcass out of the house.

The calf was certainly worth saving, as he was a strong healthy brute. In his quest for milk, he'd made it right around the carcass of his mother, tiptoeing, albeit wobbly, along on the planked floor. Ronny knew the calve's needs were first. The carcass could wait, perhaps it have to wait for awhile.

He moved to the kitchen side to cook up some bacon for breakfast, and another pot of real strong brew. The calf started bellering more, and was head butting the dead carcass. Ronny contemplated the situation, and figured that there was no way the calf could survive outside, so the thing would have to stay in, at least for the morning, until it dried off. Later he could take it out to toughen it up. Within a short while it would need food, too, and he had none. Black coffee wouldn't do. Besides, the other cows needed attention. He couldn't waste time on one critter, and risk losing the whole lot. He looked around the kitchen, decided which items he'd have to move, so the calf wouldn't destroy them, and moved them to the back room. As there was no door across between the two rooms, he propped a chair in the doorway, hoping the calf wouldn't butt it out of the way, and go crawl into bed.

After breakfast he headed outside to give the herd it's morning feed up on the hill. This time he carried along a milk bucket, planning to steal some milk from one of the two already freshened cows. The herd was waiting for him by his shack, and obediently followed him up the hill to the feeding area, except for the two calves, who stayed huddled beside his shack, safe and relatively warm from the elements. Under different conditions, an assigned babysitter cow would have stayed with them, but this place had enough smell of man about it to ward off any would be scavengers, in this case, coyotes.

He tossed the morning's allotment of greenfeed over the fence, and jumped over to spread it out. As soon as the cattle had settled into munching on the stuff, he wandered about, bucket in hand, to find the one who would be true surrogate mother.

As he approached her he spoke, and rubbed her neck, "Now, Mable, I got this problem. Elly had her calf in my shack last night. Perhaps you heard it. I have to tell you that Elly is dead, but her calf is alive, and I'm asking you to give a bit of that there fine milk of yours." He moved to the rear, bent over, and reached underneath, bucket at hand. Mable felt an unfamiliar dryness on her teat, as he tugged on it to get a little. Right now he wished it could have been Elly, as Elly had let him steal a bit, for his own use, mostly in coffee, for the last three or four years. Mable, on the other hand, was tame enough, but more nervous.

He bounced her whole udder a bit to get her more relaxed, but this was even worse than the hand on her teat, so she lifted the back leg, just to warn him, "Get the heck away from me, Mister, or I'm gonna kick your hand, and darn hard, too." Ronny had been around long enough to recognize the warning, so heeded it, and backed off. He'd have to try again later, when Mable's own little feller was having a feed.

So off he trudged, back to the shack, to see what was up with the newborn. When he arrived, he saw it, lying down beside the still warm corpse, and its face had the look of impending doom. "I'm all alone. This lump I guess is my real Mother, but she ain't moving, and I'm darn hungry." Ronny couldn't tell what it had been up to while he was out, but at least for now it was still. He went over to it, and rubbed it some more, picking some of the now dry birthing guck off of it's hair. The calf responded to him, as he would have to his own mother. At least this guy moved.

After cleaning the chap up a bit, Ronny poured himself another cup of hot coffee, and considered giving the young calf some, but didn't as he figured it would go over even worse with him than it had the night before with his mother. Then he moved to the back room, got his square bladed shovel, and went to the spot where the calf had dropped out, opened the door, and shoveled out as much of the afterbirth and mucus that he could. Fortunately for him, most of it was still within poor old Elly. He figured he'd clean the whole mess up later, when he got the carcass out, which would have to be Friday, when neighbour Pete came by.

He decided to go for another rest, until he heard the cattle arrive back from feeding. He didn't sleep well, what with the overimposing guests next door, one occasionally bellering, and the other a dead lug far too huge to budge.

Within the hour, the first two cows to arrive back were the mothers of the calves, not wanting to leave them alone for long, and also having itchy full udders that needed somebody to drain them. Ronny looked out the window to see Mable telling her calf to get up and have a suck. He threw his jacket back on, grabbed the bucket, and went out. This time she was more approachable. Her belly was full from breakfast, and Sonny boy was nursing away, so he snuck along the opposite side to the calf, reached under, and stole the milk on his side, at least as much as he thought she had. She hardly even noticed he was so unobtrusive, and she so hormone calmed from nursing and eating.

He snuck back in, passing Mable's turned head. She looked at him curiously, "What are you doing now, you old fool. I see you got the bucket again. You're not trying *that* again, are you?" But it was too late, he already had the booty.

Back inside, he poured the milk into his fake cow teat bottle with the large rubber nozzle, and took it over to the calf, who drained it all in about two minutes of voracious butting, and sucking. "Nummy," he moaned.

Ronny repeated this agenda two more times, once that evening, and again the following morning.

By Tuesday morning, the weather had cleared, and it was time to see if Mable would adopt this poor guy, as if he were a twin to the other. She'd been losing more milk for two days, and her cow milkmaking hormones had kicked in, enabling her to produce more, too. Ronny the rancher grabbed the young fellow around the middle, and hauled him outside to fresh air, sunshine, and hopefully, a surrogate mom. He snuck the willing eater to her behind, again on the opposite side, and started him on the real thing.

Mable didn't notice at first, so he got lots of her milk, enabling him to smell at least a bit like her. "Gee, this is a lot better than in there. This stuff tastes more real somehow. No rubbery taste. A lot more fun getting it, too. You get to bounce your snout off a soft warm cushiony thing." Like vine ripened real tomatoes compared to fake imported ones. He sucked her more than dry, in the gusto splendour of the moment.

Ronny watched on, in gratitude, that the calf would be okay, and that in all likelihood, Mable had adopted him. It would take two or three days to know for sure. He returned to the shed to ponder what he could do with Elly's carcass until Friday, when Pete would drop by. He pulled and tugged on her as much as he could, but without a tractor, and a couple of strong men, she was fixed to his floor, just too heavy. He considered hacking her up into pieces but couldn't bring himself to that, it being disrespectful, and a whole lot of gucky work. So he took a couple of his old blankets, and covered her up, hoping that this at least would stop some of the smell. It didn't.

He lived for the next few days in colder temperature than usual, leaving the front door open, and going outside as much as he could endure. Night time was the worst, when he snuck in around her, and stayed back in his own room, wishing he'd built a window that could be opened to get a draft. This, however would have been the first time he really needed it. Cooking was arduous at best, so other than coffee, he ate from cans, outside, in the freezing weather, away from the stench. He considered walking the five miles up to a closer neighbour than Pete, but couldn't bring himself to admit to the situation at hand. Friday couldn't come soon enough.

When Pete arrived, after the usual "Hi, Neighbour" greetings, he hung his head, and spoke of it, "Pete, I have a bit of a problem."

"What is it, Ronny? I can probably help." Pete usually could.

Might as well get this over with, he thought. "One of my cows is in my house."

"Well, can't you just chase her out." Pete didn't get the whole picture.

"Oh, no. I meant she died in my house," Ronny fessed.

"Oh, I see. What do you say we go have a look." Together they mosied over, Pete moving cautiously, as part of him really didn't want to take a look. When he did manage the courage to peek in, sure enough, Ronny had the story right. "How the heck did this happen?"

Ronny told him the story, and pointed over to the calf, now adopted. "At least that fella lived through it."

Pete chuckled to himself, and said, encouragingly, "Well, I guess I won't be getting to town quite so soon today. I'll go back, and bring down my tractor, and we can pull her out of there, I guess. Hope so anyway. Otherwise we might just have to build you a new home, Ron."

Off he drove, leaving Ronny to do naught but wait, chuckling all the way home, "Well, this has to be a gawd damn first."

The tractor arrived in an hour, with Pete driving it more like an ambulance to a rescue, than the normal way. He whipped it around, backed up to the door, jumped off, and dragged the chain as close to the carcass as he could get. "You got some rope, Ronny?"

Together they wrapped rope around her hind legs, and rolled her over so all four feet were facing up. She was stiff, and Pete had to use farmerstrength and a crowbar to reposition her, aiming her middle at the middle of the door. Before returning to the tractor, he measured with his hands, the distances across her, and across the door. "She's about a foot wider than the door, Ronny, I don't know if she's gonna go."

"Well, I sure as heck don't want to build a new house, or wreck this one.

Just get on the tractor, and try, eh?" Ronny hoped that his neighbout was a pathetic estimater of width.

But when the tractor pulled, it also stretched the stiffened muscles somewhat. Fortunately the corpse wasn't frozen, or it wouldn't have even been close. She'd have never gone. Ronny had to get the crowbar and force the swollen gut narrower at it's widest spot, but she slipped out, about as tight as the young one had slipped out of her. The old half log door bent a couple of inches on either side, but held. Pete didn't clutch to stop to talk when she exited, but kept driving, tractor transformed to hearse, up the hill to a spot out in Ronny's greenfeed field about two hundred yards away from the cattle feeding area. Elly would become coyote food. When the helpful neighbour arrived back down the hill, Ronny was standing in his doorway, having shoveled most of the leftover Elly out the door.

Pete stopped the tractor, got off, and received a "Thank You" handshake firmer than in a long time. "I'm buying coffee when we get to town," Ronny informed him.

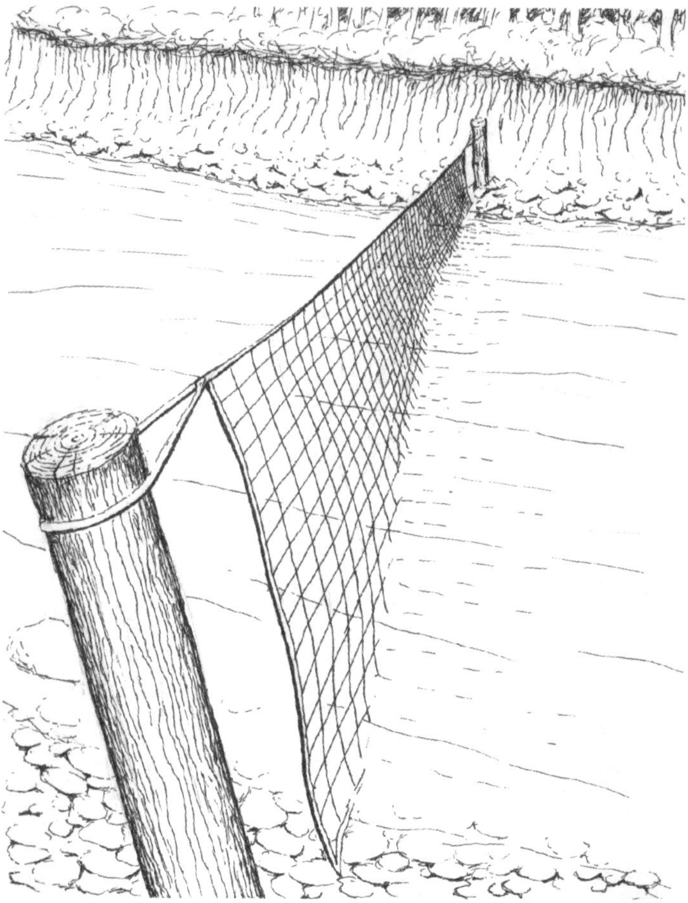

# Elmer Saves the Day

Elmer was a huge farm kid, big enough to burn diesel, weighing in at some 250 lb., and played offensive line for the local football team. One day in about 1965, Elmer was over visiting his buddy, Roy, who was a wide receiver for the same team. Roy's father, Roy, all of Roy's siblings, and friend Elmer, at the suggestion of Roy's father, decided to go down to the mouth of Grizzly Bear Creek, which meets up with the Battle somewhere out between the towns of Vermilion, and Wainwright, off some not so often travelled roads and trails. It was springtime, and this would be a likely spot to entertain a fishy with a spoon or spinner, as springtime is when fish head up the smaller creeks to find cleaner more visible water.

The Chevy half ton was able to carry the whole lot, fishing gear as well, with about four of five of the burlier fellows riding along in the back. It took about half an hour to get to the mouth. Roy's dad stopped the truck at the end of the vehicle trail, and the more enthusiastic kids piled out, and ran ahead to get to the creek's mouth first, to be first to cast a line.

Billy, the second youngest, arrived first, followed closely by Roy, and noticed the net right away. "Hey, Roy, that's a net, isn't it?" Billy wasn't sure.

"Yup, it sure is. Someone else has been coming down here." Roy replied.

"It's illegal isn't it?" Billy's curiousity was piqued.

Roy didn't know. "I think so, but let's wait til Dad gets here. He'll know for sure."

Soon Roy's dad came upon the excited scene. Kids were running about, pointing, and yelling.

Billy danced over. "Dad, someone's stretched a net across."

Dad's thoughts poured out, while all the less experienced ones listened intently, "Well, look at that. I haven't seen one since I was a kid. It's illegal now you know. In the old days it was too, but no one ever got caught." The net was stretched from one side of the creek to the other, up the creek some twenty metres or so from where it's water flowed into the river. Any fish going for a swim up into the clearer creek water would probably get tangled in it. Whoever had put it there had chosen the most suitable spot, for distance across, as well as relative proximity to the river.

Billy was curious of the technical aspects of the net. "So how did they get it across there? Did one of them have to swim?"

Dad knew his stuff. "No, they just walk back upstream a ways, where they can cross on a log or something. Then one guy goes down either side. When they get here, they throw a light rope across first, and then the guy on the other side pulls the whole net across. They tie it down, then go home, and come back every second day or so to check on it. Pretty good way of catching fish, actually, ceptin' it's illegal."

Roy expressed his disappointment. "I guess this means we won't be fishing at all. Any fish here would already be caught in the net, I guess."

Roy's dad didn't want the whole crew to be disappointed, and after a couple of more minutes of net analysis said, "Well, I guess we could check the net for them."

"But wouldn't that be illegal, Dad?" asked Billy, afraid now, not wishing to risk anything illegal.

"Well, I don't really know. It's not our net. The chances of the game warden showing up are between slim and none. If he does show up, we can just say it's not our net. Tell you what, let's not talk a lot, and if we hear a vehicle coming, we'll just put it back in really quickly."

Roy volunteered himself and Elmer. "Elmer and I will run back, and cross to the other side, so we can untie it over there. We'll stay over there until we get the thing back in." Off the football players ran, receiver ahead of the lineman. In ten minutes, they appeared through the bushes, hurried to the far side pole, and untied the net. Everyone on the original side helped pull.

"Wow. That's a huge one." yelled Billy.

"Lots of stupid suckers," Roy's Dad commented, in disgust.

"Keep pulling. Get them all out." Elmer seemed to be anxious.

Roy's Dad told Billy. "You run back to the truck, and bring those two buckets we use to sit on in the back. We can put all the fish in them."

Billy did as he was told, and then walked back up the trail to be the lookout for someone else coming along.

Within about ten minutes, the boys on the side which the net was pulled had freed twenty-four pike, ranging from about eighteen inches, to a monster that was at least ten pounds. All the tiny pike, and about a dozen suckers, were left on, for the net's owners to keep. No one ate suckers, anyway, and the teeny pike were not worth the effort of filleting.

Just as the last fish was being lifted from it's trappings, Billy, who was a little chicken anyway, and had been standing up the trail away from the excited sounds of the net removers, called out excitedly, with a twang of fear, "There's a vehicle coming! There's a vehicle coming!"

Meanwhile, that very same morning, two part Metis brothers, Richard, and Willy Youngman, had been discussing their latest food getting venture over coffee, bacon, and eggs.

"Well, Willy, should we go down the creek this morning again?" asked Richard.

Willy replied, "Yes, Richard, we should. I don't want those fish getting old. I think every second day is just right. We don't want to arouse suspicion from anyone, and the fish don't get too old that way."

Richard and Willy were technically farmers, but any new adventure or way of obtaining free food or better yet, cash, they welcomed. Making a living farming was not easy if you didn't have much land or your land was poor or you were basically lazy, and if you could supplement the legitimate cash or food with little risk of getting caught, then that was fine by them.

Besides netting from the river, they shot deer out of season, and had a tiny still for making personal moonshine. Occasionally family members or very close friends from the Metis settlement to the north would purchase some moonshine, or venison, or even fish, if the brothers could provide. Moonshine and venison were easier, because they could hunt any time during the year, and the liquor maker was way down in the river out of sight, and could be fired up any season. Fishing was seasonal, limited to the spring rush at the mouth of the creek, and occasional dynamiting of deeper holes in the fall. The legal way of using hook and line was not practical for them. It also didn't provide any thrill.

"Yup, we'd better get down there today, this morning. It might even be full already. Last time we had about twenty jack, remember." Willy wanted to go.

"You dumb guy. Of course I remember." Richard did not like the suggestion that he could not remember a mere two days back. Although he knew his memory was bad, it was not this bad. Sometimes his brother's 'smarter than you' attitude really bugged him.

"Sorry. I though maybe you had drunk too much that day," Willy kidded.

Richard didn't enjoy any kidding, and spoke seriously, "Well, I should remember. I did all the work. Took out all the fish. Filleted them all. Hung them all out to dry."

Willy gave in. "Okay. Okay." Willy, although not even a junior high school graduate, was a lot brighter, and lazier, than his brother, and was able to manipulate Richard, who was younger by two years, into most of the work, and most of the risk.

Although Richard thought the world of Willy, he didn't realize that his older brother would let him take the fall for any illegal acts without a great deal of thought. In fact, Richard would probably want to take the fall, just to keep the older brother whom he loved and admired, out of trouble.

Willy rationalized all this by reasoning to himself that if one of them were to be incarcerated, it should be the dumber one, Richard.

The boys hung out together a lot, got drunk in town, and had spent a few nights behind bars for drunk and disorderly charges. Usually it was just overnight, time enough to sober up. Bar fighting was fairly common, and both brothers knew a thing or two about winning fights. Experience had taught them well. At home, too, where they often tangled with each other. Willy usually won by outsmarting his younger opponent, even though Richard was bulkier, and stronger.

In the truck on the way down, the pair shared a ketchup bottle of their moonshine, which, after coffee, was the wake up call for the day. This got them 'off to the right start', as Willy put it. Getting a little drunk also gave them some courage for illegal acts.

"Tell you what, Richard, let's have a little bet today, on how many fish we catch. The loser has to fillet them, okay?" proposed Willy.

Richard declined, "Willy, I don't want to bet today. I always lose."

"Maybe not today," suggested Willy. This was his scheme of getting out of filleting, work, and about nine tines out of ten he could outsmart poor Richard. "You can have first guess. You get to pick. If you say ten or more, and you are right, then you have to fillet them all. If there are ten or less, then I will do it. Whatever number you pick is fine by me." Willy put the question so that if there were few, he would have to filet them but if there were lots, then Richard would have to. Richard always thought the plan was fair, because he did get to set the number. Willy always seemed to win, though. Richard felt it was just his bad luck.

"Let's see. How many did we catch last time?" Richard asked.

Willy distorted the truth. "Seventeen, exactly." In actual fact they had caught twenty, exactly.

"And how many days was the net in?" Richard always asked Willy for advice, which was Willy's plan all along.

"Two days." Willy lied a bit again, because the time before last, they had come down late in the evening, and in reality it had only been a two nights, and a day. Willy figured fish moved more by day than by night, and there would be lots today.

"Well, then, we should catch seventeen again, no, because this has been two days as well." Richard figured.

"That's right," agreed Willy, figuring his dumber brother would guess seventeen or more. Richard did not understand the game very well, or he would have just said 1000, and he would surely win. But the very thought of having to filet so many fish kept him from guessing high, and Willy knew it.

Richard thought he had it figured out. "So if I say twenty, then if there are more than twenty, I have to filet them all?"

Willy helped his brother with the logic. "Yes, that's right, but it there are less than twenty, I will filet them all."

"So we should catch about the same as last time, right."

"Yes, Richard, we should." Willy let Richard think he, Richard was doing all the thinking.

"Then I will say seventeen," said Richard.

"It's a deal." Willy shook his brother's hand, figuring he could not lose. Even if he did, he had no more than sixteen fish to filet.

Roy's dad was keen to get the net back in place, so did not bother with pulling it straight. He yelled instructions across the creek to Roy and Elmer. "Just pull it in and tie it up, quickly. Then walk back through the bushes. We want it to look like we are all on this side, in case it is the game warden. We can say it's not ours. You guys get over there and start casting out. Look like you're just here fishing. We don't want anyone to know we pulled it. Billy, get over here and help your brother take these fish way back into the bushes. Hide them in a real good spot at least a quarter of a mile from here. We'll get them later."

In the excitement of potential problems with either a game warden or with the net's owners, all the youth, and young men alike, followed Roy's dad's instructions, quickly and efficiently, keeping their voices down as much as possible. The two youngest brothers grabbed all the fish in the two buckets and scurried off into the bushes along an old cow trail. Elmer and Roy disappeared into the bushes over on the other side, having to walk back upstream to where they had crossed.

When the now partially drunk Youngman brothers arrived on the scene, all they saw was a not so old farmer, and his two young sons, leisurely casting out into the river, about ten metres beyond where they had placed the net. Being who they were, and realizing this was no game warden, they proceeded to go over to check on their two day catch.

"Richard, I think there are no good fish in here. It looks all tangled up too. I think someone's already pulled it on us." Willy was no idiot, and spoke loud enough for the farmer, and his sons to hear. Then he yelled towards Roy's Dad. "You guys been here long?"

"About half an hour."

"Had any luck catching fish."

"Nope. I think you guys probably have caught all the fish." Roy's Dad had heard of this wild brother act, but didn't know them personally. He knew enough about them that if he didn't say the right things, a fight might just break out. Not wanting to get into that, or worse, have his sons involved, he tried to be diplomatic.

"Maybe, but I don't think so. I think you bastards pulled our net. What do you think, Richard?"

"If that's what you think, Willy, then that's what I think, too." Richard never could think for himself, so just agreed with Willy. Usually if he disagreed, he got a smack or two across the back of the head, anyway. The brothers moved closer to the farmer. "You know, Mister. All we really want is our fish. I'm pretty sure you have them somewhere. The other day we were here, and there were a bunch of nice jack. Today there are just stupid suckers, and some little ones not worth keeping. That seems pretty unusual to me."

Roy's dad didn't want trouble, yet knew that these guys wouldn't stand a chance in a fight, especially if Elmer the lineman, Roy, and the two fish hiding little guys all came back. All he had to do was delay the pair a couple more minutes, "Well, first of all, your net is illegal, you know, we could tell the game warden. Secondly, we didn't pull it. Maybe some big fish got all tangled up in it and twisted it around like that."

Willy was getting frustrated, and became more aggressive. "The game warden won't know if *nobody* tells him. It would take a gawdawful big fish to wreck the net like that. Besides, what are all those footprints in the mud doing over there? Looks like your boots are a little muddy, too. So are the boots of those little kids over there. We want our fish. I'm gonna give you about one more chance to hand them over, or you're gonna get hurt."

"Well now, I don't think you want to do that. If you hurt me, then I'll have to talk to the RCMP, not just the game warden." Roy's dad was getting nervous about the approaching disaster. These fellows had little respect for the law, and from what he had heard, the older guy could care less if his little brother went to jail, anyway. Then there was the future to consider. They would find out who he was, and where he lived. Gas was easy to steal. He didn't need the trouble, really.

"Well, then, I guess you leave us no choice. My brother Richard here likes a good fight now and then. When he's drunk, he's downright nuts. Your kids are gonna get hurt, too. Not just you. All over a few measly fish. Not very smart if you ask me."

"What's going on here?" Elmer's deep voice bellowed from the trail, as he, Roy, and the two youngest siblings appeared.

Willy, and Richard turned around together, to face the 250 lb. lineman, and his not so tiny wide receiver, along with two more smaller guys. "Who the heck are you?"

"Oh, we're with them. We were just back in the bushes going for a walk up river. Who are you?" Elmer's voice remained strong.

"We live up over there somewhere, and came to check on our net. We think you guys pulled it on us."

"So what if we did." Elmer walked closer, so that the brothers' would be assaulters, could measure up better. The brothers weren't small guys, each weighing in around 200 pounds. They appeared a lot tougher, with unshaven faces, dirty clothing, and long hair. It contrasted beside Elmer, who had crewcut hair, was clean shaven, and well dressed, at least in relation to these guys.

"Well, like I was telling this guy, those are our fish you guys took." Willy had to do an abrupt turn. Now he could see that he and brother Richard were the ones that were outnumbered. This whale of a young man here, with the aid of five brothers, all young farm boys, and their father, surely would outfight he and Richard.

"So, we took your fish. They are illegally caught anyway, and there isn't much you can do, is there?" Elmer had the upper hand. He wanted no part of any fight, being a gentle giant actually, but also knew his size alone *was* intimidating.

Willy took another look around, counting heads, checking out the twisted net, and pondering the situation one last time, kicking the ground all the while, like a rooster. Eventually his eyes settled on his brother, "Well, Richard, I think you and I might as well go home. There ain't much point in staying here now. No fish, no fun. These people have ruined the day."

"Yes, Willy, I can see that, too. We might as well go home." Richard echoed.

Together the pair headed dejectedly for the truck. Elmer looked at Roy, "I think we should tag along just so they don't wreck the truck, or anything."

"Good idea." Elmer and Roy followed along just to be sure.

Brothers Youngman got into their truck dejectedly. Richard grumbled profanities as he kicked the passenger side rear front tire on the way to get in. Willy sped off, dusting up the trail by spinning the tires, and nearly hitting the ditch.

Richard realized that there was something good about this, even if it was just for him, not the pair of them "Hey, Willy. I guess this means I won the bet. Since the number of fish is less than seventeen, you have to filet them all."

"Shut up, Richard. For sure I'll filet all ZERO of the goldarned fish we have. Is there any moonshine left?"

Back at the creek, the farmer and his crew were busy loading their illegal catch of pike onto the truck. It was the their largest haul ever. Mother would be proud. Roy's Dad instructed them all, "We caught these fish all on rod and reel. Right, boys?"

"Right, Dad."

# Next Week

One Sunday, during a mediocre cycle of fishing in the Battle, an ol' farmer part time fisherman named Red McAllister decided he would impress his four young 'uns of the roads and trails he remembered along the Battle that lead to fishing holes just waiting to be cleaned out, 'if a fellow brought along the right equipment', so got up, fried his bacon and eggs, and informed the lads.

"I'm going fishing today, boys. Who wants to come?"

"I do," said Flipper the youngest.

"Me, too," added Smartso, the oldest.

"Me, too," said Curious Joe, the second oldest, not wanting to be left out.

"Will we have to walk anywhere?" inquired Lazyhead, second youngest.

"Nope, we'll take the truck." Red was prepared.

"Then me, too." Lazyhead was okay with this.

"How about sister?" Red looked at his daughter as he asked, knowing he should at least offer up the opportunity.

"Nope. Fishing is a boy thing," she replied. This would be a break from the damn rascals.

"Mom?" asked Flipper.

"Nope. I have too much work today, but you fellows run along now. Have fun. Here's the lunch I packed." At least the five males would be out of her hair for the day, and she might actually get ahead a bit.

Curious Joe, asked, curiously, "Mom, how did you know we were going fishing?"

"Sometimes Dad and I talk about these things, you know," she informed him.

"Oh." Curious Joe was satisfied, as was the case usually, with Mom's responses.

So into the truck they hopped, Red, having just purchased two brand new rod and reel sets, and a few leaders, and lines, having just rediscovered that very summer that, "The fish are back. The fish are back!"

"Don't sit on the fishing gear, boys. I want to catch something, and if you wreck it all, we won't catch a thing," he ordered, sargeant like.

Lazyhead and Flipper, the youngest young 'uns, hopped into the cab of the ol' '49, and the older two hopped into the back. Dirtboy, the mongrel shepherd/collie jumped in with them but he got tossed, poor ol' chap. Smartso explained the decision to the mongrel, "Dirtboy, you have to stay home this time. We're all gonna be too busy fishing to look after a dirty dog."

Ears and eyes were never more alive as the Chevy headed out, for none of the lads had ever caught a single fish, their only experience proudly watching a washtub full of still half-alive jumpers brought back by Papa from some northern lake, which had whetted their appetite for the fishing experience, and the river was only a few miles off. The half ton's back window was open, as normal, so Red could yell, if necessary, to the back.

"How many do you think we'll catch?" put forth Curious Joe.

"Hundreds." Flipper didn't know numbers.

"Thousands." Lazyhead knew exaggeration.

"Probably just one or two tiny ones." Smartso was a realist.

"I'm gonna catch me a huge one." Curious Joe was dreaming aloud.

Red spoke, kids listened, "We'll be lucky if we get one. But it'll be fun, all day. We'll see some trail anyway." He made it sound like a no lose situation.

"I hope each of us catches at least one. What do you think, Dad?" Smartso desired success for all.

"Let's just wait and see." Dad was not sure.

"Okay," agreed Smartso.

"By the way, where are we going, Dad?" inquired Lazyhead.

Red explained his plan, "Down an old road on the east side that follows Uncle's pasture for a bit, and then keeps going along the river. There used to be some homesteads down there, but they all shut down. I'm not even sure if the road is open, but we'll try. We're going to an old fishing hole I heard about called the Macklin hole."

"How come it's called that?" asked Flipper.

"I guess the homesteader was named Macklin," Red explained.

"Figures," said Smartso.

"Wow, a road that isn't even open. This ought to be fun. We'll probably get stuck." Lazyhead showed his pessimistic side.

"How far does this road go, Dad?" asked Curious Joe.

"It used to go all the way to the next bridge, about 10 miles over, as the crow flies." Dad knew his geography.

"Okay!" yelled Flipper, excited.

Sure enough, Papa was right. The road could still be traversed, albeit somewhat doubtfully at times. There were a few fallen trees to remove from the path, but with four eager strongsters around that was easy. Several gates to neighbour pastures needed opening but always a willing youngster popped out of the cab or the back, and got it. One particular spot scared the bedevil out of the whole fishing crew. The trail passed precariously close to the bank of the river, some 30 feet higher than the river bed. To make matters worse, the old trail wasn't level at that point, but leaned towards the precipice, so that it gave a sensation that just a bit more would have the truck not just flipping on its side but also rolling over and down to the river edge, if not splashing into the river itself. From the back, Curious Joe, a would be daredevil, leaned over, "Whoa. Look at that! I can see water almost straight down!"

The others, including the leader/teacher/father breathed a collective sigh of relief as the truck passed by, and regained its level. "Whew."

Ol' Red vowed, "Next time I'm bringing an axe. We'll bust out a new bypass road around this spot. No use killing ourselves over a few darn fish."

"Next time?" queried Flipper.

"Yuppee, even if we don't catch a fish, there will be a next time." Curious Joe was joyous with the news.

Finally the key was turned and the engine rumbled to a silence, broken by Red's announcement, "This is it. We're here! Don't know if we'll make it back home or not, but we're here for now. Let's go fishing!"

The hole was just as Papa had described it to the boys, and soon the two lines were being cast out, and eagerly reeled back in. The five fisherman shared the two lines eagerly and fairly, as sharing was part of the way of family farming, not a problem, as they were all used to it. One line would have been sufficient. They could tell by the darkness of the water that Papa was right, this was a deep hole, probably at least ten feet, maybe more. No doubt this place had fish, beautiful long hungry fish lurking in those depths. Alas, after half an hour of futility, Lazyhead, tired now, asked, "Well, what are we gonna do now, Dad, go home?"

Red, not a quitter, looked Lazyhead down. "Are you kidding, son? We just got here. There are more holes than this one in these parts. This river has all kinds of holes. You just have to be willing to move about a bit is all." He stood back, and climbed to a higher perch. He called down to Smartso, and Flipper, who were sharing one rod. "Okay. See that rapid over there. Fish just love to hide right below the rapid and sneak out. Go cast over there right where still water meets rushing water. You'll catch one for sure."

Flipper doubted the proposition. "For sure?"

Red responded truthfully, "Well, nothing's for sure, son, but you have to try."

Flipper and Smartso mosied over to the rapid, but alas, to their disappointment, once again each hook cast out greeted only water. Occasionally a rock or some algae would latch on, and Smartso would have to wade in a bit to unsnag it, but nothing even half resembling a fish took a bite.

"There ain't no fish over here, either, Dad. That one you caught earlier was probably the only one in this whole darn river," yelled Smartso, pointing out a seemingly logical possibility.

"Oh, I don't think so. We just have to keep trying." Ol' Red was determined to teach some diligence, if nothing else.

"But, Dad, these holes are small. If there was a fish in there, don't you think after about 100 casts, you'd have caught one," Lazyhead continued the dispute on behalf of Smartso.

Red, who was enjoying the view, despite the lack of nibbles, went on with another possibility, "Well sometimes maybe they're on the move, and one might come into the hole just as you're leaving. That would be disappointing now, wouldn't it?"

Flipper agreed, but wished more, "Yeah, I guess. I want to try somewhere else."

Red called,"Okay, then. There's another hole just upstream about a quarter of a mile. We might as well try that one before we go home. It's a bit of a walk, though."

"Walking? I thought you said we wouldn't have to walk." Lazyhead wasn't happy with this turn of events.

"We drove all the way here, didn't we?" Dad knew Lazyhead could be turned via logic..

Lazyhead had hit the unexpected. "Yeah, but now we have to walk?"

Red was getting a bit dissed, "Just a bit. Do you want fish or not?"

"Well, yeah, I want fish. That's what we came for," answered Lazyhead.

Red explained further, "Real fishermen have patience, and will walk about a bit."

"Let's just leave Lazyhead here, Dad. The rest of us will come," said Curious Joe.

Lazyhead, not wanting to be the straggler, abruptly changed his tone, was won over, for now. "Okay, then, let's go," he said, sounding like it was his idea all along.

A quarter mile of bush and cowpaths had the bunch of still mostly optimistic fellows come out along a steep but short bank, which had a few trails going down every few feet or so, but had precarious standing at the water's edge, eight feet below the rim of the bank. At the bottom of one path lay a beaver house, half dug into the bank, half extended out into the water. The beavers along here made full use of nature's gift, a bank.

"Might have to get our shoes wet a bit here, but I think this is the spot," Ol Red informed them, as they scrambled over the edge, having to turn around and let themselves hang over the grassy edge, and seek out footholds with searching roving feet, and pass the fishing gear down. Soon all five were perched along on clumps of grass knobs or the edge of the beaver house.

Smartso, the observant, observed, "Looks like a good spot, but it's so hard to cast out because of the bank."

"That's why your hook is set in that tree behind you," Lazyhead chuckled.

"I guess," agreed Smartso, unhappily.

"I think I got one! I think I got one!" Flipper yelled.

"What does it feel like?" Red, the teacher/expert, offered his help, but wasn't sure if the kid could tell a rock or a snag from a fish.

"It feels like I got one!" Flipper screamed again.

"Is it pulling back a bit on you?" asked Red, wanting to know if indeed it was a fish.

"It feels like I got one!" repeated Flipper.

"Well, start reeling it in," advised the master.

"What?" Flipper just didn't inderstand.

"Start reeling it in," repeated his father, slower.

Finally Flipper calmed down enough to understand. "Oh, now I get it!" he called, as he started reeling.

Ol' Red had to be commander, teacher, and gentle advisor, but would have to get soaked to get to where his youngest son had hooked the first fish, ever. "Not too hard. It'll get away if you pull too hard. Be gentle. Someone else get the heck over there and help him land it."

"What do you mean?" asked Lazyhead.

"Help him!" commanded Red.

"How?" asked Lazyhead, honestly, as he had no clue.

"Grab the leader. That's the thing right beside the hook. It's stronger." Red had insufficient time to explain, "I knew I should have brought a net," he sighed.

"What's a net?" asked Curious Joe, who was standing beside his dad.

"Never mind. Let's just help him with the fish."

Together, Lazyhead, and Flipper, in competition to see whose eyes could get wider, landed the foot long pike. "What a beauty!" exclaimed Lazyhead.

"And I caught it!" added Flipper.

"It's got a huge mouth," observed Smartso, who had crawled back up the bank, and then back down, so he could observe more closely.

"And I caught it!" yelled Flipper.

"It sure swallowed the hook," said Lazyhead.

"And I caught it!" yelled Flipper, again.

"How do you get the hook out, Dad?" asked Smartso.

"And I caught it!" Louder now, the youngest *needed* to have everyone acknowledge this.

There was a strange silence. Then a chorus of mixed voices rang out, almost simultaneously, "Yes, Flipper, you caught it!"

Papa got over there, and helped to remove the hook. More fish were coming. Another couple of hours casting at the same hole, and collectively the fishermen five caught a grand total of eight fish: six pike, and two walleye. The only person skunked was Daddy the expert, but this was no problem, because after all, that was the teacher's role. He taught the boys how to make a stringer out of a branch, how to keep the fish in water to keep them fresh, and how to make sure they didn't get away. He didn't have to teach them how to brag, as that seemed to come rather natural, as Mother found out, upon arrival home.

"I caught the first one," said Flipper.

"I caught one of the walleye," added Curious Joe.

"Mine was the biggest!" bragged Lazyhead.

"Dad didn't catch any," said Smartso.

"Mine fought the hardest," said Curious Joe.

Flipper, not to be outdone, continued, "But my second one fought the longest."

Father, as well, taught them, at least those that could stomach it, with much assistance from Mother, how to fillet the things, now that they were home, shown to Chief cook, as if it were a primeval tribal duty of mankind, to let the women butcher. "Didn't have a filletting knife with us, Dear. Didn't know we were going to catch any. Besides, they're easier to fillet when they've hardened up a bit, eh?" Red excused himself from doing most of the sordid ritual of gutting.

Whether or not Mother and Sis were actually interested or just polite was unimportant. The fact of the matter was that Dad had been correct. There *WERE* fish in that there river, and by gosh, they all knew how to catch them now. It wasn't long before the inevitable came up.

"Dad, when can we go again?" asked Curious Joe.

"Yeah, Dad, when can we go again?" added Lazyhead.

"Yeah, Dad, that was fun. When can we go again?" repeated Flipper.

Smartso couldn't resist getting in on it, "You might even catch one this time, if we EVER go again."

The poor fellow probably felt intimidated, or that he wasn't up to his duties to teach these things as a true father would, so barely soon enough to shut the boys up, the anticipated words fell out, "Next Sunday, boys. Next Sunday."

Next Sunday did not arrive soon enough. The week was spent preparing. The two rigs were cleaned, and polished, while casting practice on the yard almost wore them out. Old nuts from some old nutty farm machinery served as weights for the practice. It was fortunate that the two cheap rigs had any life left for the next Sunday what with all the practicing that occurred.

Ol' Red even made a special trip to town to have each young 'un pick out a favorite shiny new hook, and held his tongue when he 'knew' that a particular hook wouldn't catch a darn thing.

Sunday morning finally rolled along, and no one had to be yelled at to get up.

"Well boys, I see you're all ready for another great day down there. We're more ready this time. I know we're gonna catch a bunch. I think we can stop at a few different holes along there, too."

"We're ready." Flipper and Lazyhead beamed collectively.

"I got the fishing stuff in there already." Smartso added, responsibly.

"Tackle box and all?" asked Red, not willing to concede a total preparation on their part.

"Yup. She's all ready to go," confirmed Smartso

"Did Mom pack us a lunch again?" asked Lazyhead.

Red answered, with confidence, "Nah. We're fishermen, remember. I'm just taking along a filleting knife, a frying pan, a bit of bread, and some butter. We're having fish for lunch!"

"Great! Did you remember matches?" asked Smartso, wishing his father hadn't remembered, so he, Smartso, could be the one who was more prepared

"I guess we'll bring all the rest home, won't we?" said Curious Joe, assuming the catch would be marvellous.

"Yup. That's the plan. We'd never be able to eat all the fish we're going to catch." Red insisted.

"Yessir!" yelled Flipper, with joyous enthusiasm, but not fully understanding. 'Yessir' was just something you said at times like these.

Red looked at the four boys, and asked, "Then what are we waiting for?"

Out to the truck, a brief stop at the farm gas tank for gas, and the anglers five were off again, seeking an even more profound rerun of last week's adventure.

"How many do you think we'll catch this week?" propositioned Curious Joe.

"I think about 20. I'll say exactly 23. We have better equipment now," guessed Lazyhead.

"Dad said we're stopping at more holes, so I'm gonna say 16," said Curious Joe.

Smartso guessed, too, "I say five of each. That's probably really gonna be real low, but I don't want to take chances. I'm still not sure about last week. It's still hard for me to believe, having lived here all this time, and never catching fish down there before."

"What do you think, Dad?" asked Flipper, needing advice.

"Well, obviously we will catch fish. We caught eight last week, and they say it gets better as fall wears on. The water is even clearer than last week, and we'll check out a couple more holes. I got you guys four new hooks, and some better leaders, and now we have experience. Gee, I think your mother's gonna be surprised when we come home for supper." Red had it figured, from a week of thinking.

The road hadn't changed, and Red forgot to bring the axe he'd vowed to bring, he was so caught up in the excitement of the fishing with the boys, so once again the old truck had to pass by the scary precipice on the narrow trail with gasps or "Whew" loud enough to wake the fish sleeping below.

The week long rest from fishing left them refreshed, at least for fishing, so the crew skipped the first two fishless holes of the prior week. Instead they hurried back to the same spot where Lady Luck had allowed all eight creatures to be taken.

Alas, after an hour or so, there were no nibbles, not even a peep, or a fish shaped rock, and the boys tired of the lack of success.

"Well, Dad, I'm hungry." Flipper threw in the fishing towel, quicker than any other.

Red looked at the youngest boy with pity, but would not heed the whine. "All we have is the bread. I think we should save it for awhile yet, so that when we catch fish, we'll have something to go with the fish."

"Okay," said Flipper, reluctantly. Another hour passed before he repeated, "Dad, I'm hungry."

This time Dad was more approachable. "Well, I'm a little hungry, too. I guess we might as well all share the bread we have. If we do catch a fish or two, we can still fry them up. Don't put the butter on the bread."

"This bread is dry," whined Lazyhead.

"Too bad. That's all we have." Red was not about to hear such minor complaints.

'Better than nothing," observed Smartso.

Curious Joe, too expessed his agreement with Lazyhead. "Not a whole lot," he said.

"If you don't like it so much, why don't you just go over there, and catch a darned fish?" suggested Smartso.

"Why don't you, Bigmouth?" muttered Lazyhead.

"Isn't bigmouth a kind of fish,Dad?" asked Curious Joe.

"No, it's a kind of person, like you," said Lazyhead, being angry from hunger.

So five forlorn looking disappointed fellows huddled around a circle of rocks, and a roaring fire, bemoaning and groaning about the fact that the river had not been kind, and the poor frying pan would not be able to fulfill it's god-given destiny of companionship with a fillet of fresh fish. A few more casts in two or three spots soon led them all to believe that the Mother, Nature, was not about to give in, and that today was a day that they would just he to suffer the fate of many an overly optimistic fisherman before them, and probably just as many after them.

Lazyhead pointed his finger at Red. "It's Dad's fault. He should have known better."

Red defended himself, "Come on now, any one of us could have packed a lunch."

Flipper yawned, and begged to them all, "I'm hungry. Let's just go home."

But Red persisted, "Maybe the very next cast will get a fish, a whopper, bigger than any of last week."

"I doubt that very much," said Lazyhead.

"We should have brought some food," declared Smartso.

"We're so stupid!" exclaimed Curious Joe.

Smartso retaliated, "Speak for yourself. I'm not stupid."

"I still say it's Dad's fault. At least he should have known better," repeated Lazyhead.

Flipper looked up at Dad, and begged, again, "I'm hungry, Dad. Let's just go home."

But Red disagreed, "We can't go home like this. Your mother will laugh at us." He feared it would become another of those, "Remember when..." lifetime stories his wife liked to bring up, when he bragged of any outdoor adventure to relatives or neighbours.

Flipper didn't care. "I don't care how much Mom laughs. I'm hungry."

"Right now I could eat a horse!" Curious Joe exaggerated.

"I could eat a fish," said Lazyhead, wishfully.

Smartso had had enough of Lazyhead, "Shut up. You can't eat a fish if you can't catch a fish."

Lazyhead glared back, "Well, neither can you, you stupid kid."

"Look who's calling who stupid. At least I didn't predict 23 stupid fish."

"Yeah, you only said 10. What's the difference?" Lazyhead pointed out the trivial detail. None was none. That was that. Any number beyond none would have been historically significant.

Flipper broke the potential brotherfight, saying "Dad, how come you did this to us? Is this your idea of a joke? Well, if it is, it sure isn't very funny. Let's just go home, please?"

McAllister gave in this time, but not without raising the future, "Well, okay, Flipper. You're right. We'll just go home empty handed. I'll be back one day though, and teach those darn fish a lesson."

Finally, after the long miserable day, jeans spoiled from spending some 7 or 8 hours trudging through bush and bramble, eyes smoked out from fire, arms aching from endless casting, feet tired from alternating wet and dry, and stomachs growling from shrinkage, the futile sorrowful lot dragged themselves back up to the farmstead, to be met by a still optimistic mother, and wife.

"Well, my boys, let's see what you caught today," she smiled.

"Mom, I hate to tell you this, but we caught nuthin," frowned Flipper.

"Nuthin at all?" asked Mom, looking at the poor bedraggled creature.

"Nuthin at all," he reiterated.

"Not even a minnow, or a little jack," she continued, in disbelief.

"Nuthin, Mom, nuthin." Poor Flipper was taking it hard.

"All you boys don't seem too happy about this. This sure is a bit of a turnaround from last week, eh?" Mom began to smile.

Curious Joe answered for them all. "I guess it is, Mom, yes. I'm hungry. What's for supper?"

"Well, seeing as it's Sunday and all, and I never did trust that guy that took you boys fishing on things like this, I threw in extra vegetables, and a bigger roast than normal. I figure it should be just about ready now."

Curious Joe complimented her. "Geez, Mom, you're smart."

"Well, smarter than your dad, anyway." She gave him a self satisfied look.

Red had few choices but to wither in self-pity, "Hey, it was just an unlucky day. All fishermen have their unlucky days. Who wants to try their luck next week?"

"Not me," said Flipper, emphatically.

"Me neither," agreed Lazyhead.

"You go ahead, Dad," said Smartso.

Curious Joe wasn't quite as sure, "Well, are you going to take a lunch this time, or are you just taking the frying pan?" he asked.

"I think maybe I'll take a lunch," replied Red. "You know, maybe there's a big monster one just waiting for you. You kids just give up too easily."

# Water Intake

The Battle provides water to several communities along its course. At these spots, a damn is first constructed to create a small reservoir that will ensure a water depth sufficient for year round intake, and then once the man-made lake is complete, the rest of the construction can be completed. Usually a water purification plant is established nearby, and there is an elaborate safety built in, with screens over the intake, and the whole area being fenced off, so that no would-be vandal could pull any mischief. A whole community may depend on this system, and small town mayors argue about who has the superior tasting water. Even though it's all Battle water, politicians are politicians, and will create all sorts of stories to dupe the local electorate. The fence is there for safety, being that the dam is flat, and although walkable, often becomes slippery with small algae growth. The water is deep only on the upstream side. The overflow concrete pad takes the water away at a mild slope, the water eddying a bit as it bottoms out. Were it not for the safety fence, these structures would surely be used for innertubing and play.

The only problem is that these water intake sites become safe havens for fish, because of the water depth, and daring or stupid fishermen will scale the fence just to cast a line, in such a likely spot, albeit man made. Not as daring or unethical as cutting a hole in the fence of a game reserve, but illegal all the same. If it were not for the fact of these places being fish havens, the temptation wouldn't exist. But fishermen are fishermen, and the idea of pulling in a huge walleye or pike remains irresistible. The chances of getting caught are remote, as the water plant, where people work, is usually located up on the hill plain overlooking the valley, as the intake system becomes nearly maintenance free once it's installed.

With the potential of horsing in a fat walleye in mind, Stan, full of typical fisherman false optimism, decided to take his wife and daughter out to one such location, and capture one of those 'delicious monsters' lurking in the reservoir's depths. "Marge," he said, "Whaddya say we take Small Fry there fishing today?"

"It's okay with me," Marge agreed, hoping he wouldn't be going to his illegal spot, but figuring that's what he meant.

Janey looked up from her breakfast, and said, "I want to come, too."

"Of course you can come, Dear," Marge reassured the three year old. Then she turned to Stan, "Where are you planning to go?"

"To my usual spot, of course." This meant he wished to poach from the reservoir.

"I don't know. What if we get caught?" Marge didn't mind so much his going alone, but for him to insist his family come along, now that was different.

"I want to go," said Janey, for the umpteenth time in her life. She was like a farm dog that way. She *always* wanted to go: for a drink at the tavern, to a welding site, to the bank to borrow money, to an outhouse at a park, up a tree. Not being around other kids much, she saw herself as a mini-adult, and became a tagalong, participating child-like in innappropriate contexts. She was one of those kids that childless people hate, yet tolerate, in order to do business with her parents.

"I'm going to catch you a monster," he boastfully predicted to Janey.

"I don't like monsters, Daddy. They're scary."

Marge intervened, "A monster is just a saying for a big fish, Dear."

She had the choice of not going, putting up with being alone with Janey for the morning, or tagging along with this guy on *his* adventure. Marge decided, hesitantly, but didn't let him know. "When are we leaving, then?"

For him, illegality was not really an issue, compared to the likelihood of feasting on walleye. Even should they be caught, the probable penalty was simply to be asked to leave. Fishing in the Battle wasn't illegal, just the trespassing was. The men who worked the water plant could fish here all the time, with no such trouble. Their private fishing hole, owned by the public, not unlike the private fishing holes of Wabamun's steam power plant, except that here one has to actually fish. At Lake Wabamun, the fish enter the much larger intake system on their own, only to be tossed back into the lake, by an already sick of free fish, worker.

Stan pulled the truck up to the end of the road, on the river's opposite side to the plant, and walked down a trail known only to the locals. "The fish are waiting for me, Dear. I can tell." It had been some time since he'd done this, so he was anticipating it. It was his favorite, almost only, fishing spot, as he had never been skunked here. The valley scenery, the rebellious thrill of fence jumping, and the admiring company he kept, all added to his optimistic, self satisfied view of the world, especially today's view.

"We're coming, Dear," Marge called, as she followed him along the path, Janey in tow.

"Daddy's going to catch us a fish, isn't he, Mommy?" babbled the three year old girl, long brown hair flowing behind her, as she struggled to keep pace, with Mom.

"Yes, he is, Dear," Marge assured her, she too optimist regarding that likelihood. Marge didn't fish, just preferring to let her man do it all, and watch. She cooked the things, and fresh walleye made superb meals.

"Will it be a big fish, Mommy?" Janey looked up at the perky fresh aired face of her mother.

"We don't know until he catches it," Marge replied honestly.

"Will we eat the fish, Mommy?"

"Yes, Janey, we will eat the fish."

When the family got to the fence, Stan poked his rod and reel under first, and then boosted his wife up and over. Grabbing his not so heavy three year old with one arm, he climbed up, and handed the child to the ever loving arms of her mother, on the other side. Then he too climbed over, jumping from near the top, and landing on uneven ground, twisting his ankle. "Damn," he blurted, unimpressed with his inability to become a fit soldier in warfare scaling a fence built by Nazis.

"Wow, Daddy jumped!" gleamed the girl, not realizing she had witnessed a quasi-illegal act, or that Daddy was hurt. At age three, parents are Gods, and legal questions, or parental injuries are nowhere even close to entering the self-centered mind. All Janey knew was that she was having fun, oblivious to any moral judgments, or injury to Daddy.

Stan limped in the direction of the nearest tree, "Gotta drain the dragon," he informed Marge of the purpose for a slight delay.

"Is Daddy catching a Dragon?" Janey asked her mother, thinking the adventure was only beginning now, imagining a fierce dragon lurking somewhere over there in those bushes.

"No, Dear, he's just going to the washroom," Marge explained.

"How come he said he was draining a dragon?"

"It's just a saying men have for when they go to the washroom, Dear."

"Oh," Janey giggled, "that's funny."

The family scrambled down the bank to the edge of the weir. Water was flowing across the top, at a depth today of only an inch. It had been constructed in alternating up and down two foot sections, with a height difference of three inches between each section, so that at least in low flow, there were steps that could be traversed easily. The top part was six feet across so each dry platform was two feet by six feet, ideal spots to sit on to enjoy the scene. Some thirty or more such platforms crossed the river in a straight line to the other side. Danger on top was minimal today. Only during higher flow, when the platforms themselves, were submerged, did real danger in crossing exist. The upstream side fell straight off at a near vertical angle of some 60 degrees. Bits of dead algae, sand, and grit clung to most of the many concrete corners. The structure never needed cleaning as each spring, in high flow, the Battle's force would swish it all away.

Marge held her daughter while Stan calmly traversed the platforms to the other side, where he could get a decent casting position a few yards upstream, from the shore, and where he would have plenty of room to land the monsters. He talked to them as he crossed. "I hope you little stupid fishy fishies are ready. Papa's gonna catch one of you poor suckers for his baby. Better watch out for those spoons. If you had any clues, you'd get the hell out of here. Supper is walleye tonight. You guys are $%#@! stupid, and I'm going to prove it. You're not supposed to be here in this illegal place. Neither am I, but I'm smarter, and I'm going to remover you $%#@^&&s from this water. If you think you can outsmart ol Stan here, you're fooling yourselves."

Janey heard him, and asked, "Mommy, who's Daddy talking to?"

"The fish, Dear. He's talking to the fish," she explained.

"Can the fish hear him, Mommy?" Her inquisitive eyes beckoned for a "Yes" answer, as then it would be just like some of the books Mommy had read to her.

"No, Dear. I suppose the fish might hear him, but they can't understand." She reflected how talking to fish made somewhat more sense than talking to the Blue Goose, his truck, when it misbehaved, or cursing the golf balls, "You little %$#$%$#," just before he swung. At least the fish were animate, and had ears, unlike the other inanimate machines he carried on conversations with. At least today he wasn't talking vulgar, in angry or threatening tones. He was being somewhat amiable to the fish. The truck, or the golf balls got downright foul language some days, when they did not obey.

"Then why is he talking to them, Mommy, if they can't hear?" Janey was persistent.

"I guess he thinks it brings him better luck. Daddy is also used to talking to himself," Mommy explained more.

Janey was satisfied now, and began a new line of questioning, "Can we go out closer, Mommy, where we can watch him better?"

"Yes, we can go out on those square islands, but you will have to let Mommy carry you, and be real careful when we stop." Marge was only slightly wary of the situation. Janey usually followed her instructions to a tee, and these islands were dry and flat.

"We can see Daddy much better, then, right, Mommy?" She was observant for her age.

"Yes, Dear, we will have the best seat in the house." Marge had wanted to go out on the weir all along, but was afraid to just pick Janey up and carry her, because if Janey were to be afraid, she might struggle. On the other hand, if Janey suggested it herself, her three year old independence would not allow to back down from any fear that might come up later.

"Mommy, this isn't the house." Janey stated, with a confused look.

"The best seat in the house is just a saying, Dear, that means we have a very good spot to watch from," Marge explained.

"Oh. Like when Daddy said 'drain his dragon'." Janey was easy to explain sayings to. Marge's teacher background aided. She had confidently explaining stupid English idioms to grade ones for quite a while, never 'drain the dragon', or 'seduce the canine', though. She hadn't written a list of vulgar adult idioms on the board to go over one by one, thankfully.

Soon the mother-daughter pair arrived midstream, just at the point where Stan's casts were landing. The watchers were closer to the hook's splash than the caster was. If he did latch on to one out there, they would have a clearer view than he. "Look, Mommy, you can see Daddy's hook. It makes a splash," Janey admired.

"I think we should sit down here for awhile, Janey. We can watch Daddy catch one." Marge set her daughter down on one of the concrete rectangles, and stepped over to the adjacent one to sit down herself, to enjoy the day watching her spouse attempting to entice one in, from truly the best view in the house.

After about fifteen minutes of watching Daddy cast, the wee girl started becoming squiggly, and moved closer to the water's edge to peer curiously into the depths. "This place is like that story, Mommy." Janey was always making connections between bedtime stories, and life.

"Which story is that?" Marge asked.

"You know." Janey always assumed her Mommy knew everything, even Janey's own thoughts. Especially stories.

"No, honest, I don't know. Tell me more." Marge enjoyed Janey's ability to connect life and fiction, even if there was some distortion.

"The one with that funny name, and the little boy, and all those pretty fish," explained Janey.

Marge deciphered the clues. Only one answer could be correct, of the many books she had read, "Oh, you mean, "McElligot's Pool?"

"That's the one. Gelligot's Pool. Will Daddy catch a fish that has two heads, or an umbrella fish?"

"No, Dear. If Daddy catches a fish it will be an ordinary fish." Marge secretly wished differently. An umbrella fish would be a whole lot more fascinating than a walleye. Perhaps she wouldn't have to gut an umbrella fish.

Stan's hook landed about ten feet out in front of Janey, and sunk into the depths, as Stan was allowing it to do, letting it sink to near the bottom, where he figured the cursed walleye lie waiting. Janey watched it disappear from her sight, until she saw a flash of white, indicating that Mr. Walleye hadn't listened to Daddy's threats, having chewed a sharp hook rather than some delicious morsel.

There was no verbal indication from Stan that he had one on, as he held the superstition of never letting anyone know he had a fish on, until he landed it. He felt yelling always brought bad luck in bringing them to shore. 'Brag only when the job is over' was his superstitious motto. In the walleye's effort to cough up the hook, it veered over in Janey's direction, pulling the line along, and forcing Stan's rod to tip, almost breaking.

Marge's back was turned, as she, now bored with the endless casting, was admiring the little rivulets and swirls that occurred at the bottom of the spillway on the down side of the dam. She pondered how deep the water was there, and imagined being younger, sliding down the concrete slide, with several childhood friends, and handsome farm lads, their muscles reeking of testosterone, and mouths uttering false bravado.

Janey, curious, but naive three year old she was, leaned over closer to have a superior look at the struggling fish, but leaned too far, lost her not so good in the first place balance, and summersaulted directly into the water, head first. Her momentum forced a splash, and she summersaulted, completely underwater, as in an overturned swan dive, her nose breathing in the liquid, as though she had transformed into the walleye's kin. Within five seconds, her brown hair surfaced first, as she floated back up, splashing about with her tiny hands, jacket saturated, and pulling her down. She felt the cold on her skin, and hollered a muffled, "Mommy!"

On the moment of the splash, in catlike reflex only attributed to motherhood, Marge whirled around in time to see the ending of the spin, and the brown hair afloat. By the time she scrambled the six feet back, her child, her only child, had disappeared for the second time below the surface, instinct having taken over, in a valiant struggle to breathe. Marge reached down to grab the jacket's hood, and held on. She tried to pull the toddler up, but as she tugged, her hold became a stranglehold, so for the moment, all she could do was hold Janey's head safely above water. "Are you okay, Dear?" she asked.

The child, still unnerved by the incident, replied, "I'm swimming, Mommy."

Not wishing to spoil the child's distorted view by argument, Marge answered, "Yes, Dear, you sure are. I'm going to hold on to you until Daddy comes, okay?" Then she yelled, "Stan, can you come over here. I need some help!" Marge figured she might not be strong enough to pull the hunk of wet clothes containing a body, or that she might tumble in herself.

From shore, Stan saw the disastrous splash, and had witnessed Marge turn to grip their child. Now, this was a dilemma. "Hmmmm," he thought. "shall Mr. Fish come to shore, or shall Superman save the girl?" Such decisions for fishermen. Fortunately for Janey, Daddy wasn't one of those true blue hard-core wacko joke guys, who'd clearly go for the fish first, daughter second. He stuck the rod's handle end into the sand, and then frustrated that he couldn't run full out because of his fence jumping injury and the treacherous weir, began the hero's journey to save a life.

"Hurry up!" she called again.

"I'm coming as fast as I can!" he yelled to reassure her of the impending rescue.

When he approached, he saw Marge in the precarious position of holding her daughter's head above water, while maintaining her own balance.

"I don't have a very good grip on her," Marge explained.

Superman Stan had to analyse the situation, quickly. Either risk Marge going in as well, or losing her grip, and having the Small Fry go in deeper, or go in himself. Tough job for Stan, Stan, the fisherman. "Then I'm going in," he informed his wife of the momentous decision.

"Goody, Daddy's coming swimming with me. That'll be more fun." said Janey, feeling left out of the conversation, and looking forward to a swimmer companion.

Fortunately for Janey, her Daddy could swim. He didn't feel he had time to bother to remove any clothing at all, but recognized that his boots would be the enemy once he got in, so hurriedly removed them, then slipped in feet first, about two metres to the side of Janey. Diving would have meant an abrupt encounter with concrete. 'SUPERMAN HITS HEAD ON CONCRETE, DIES!' read the headline. As he slid down the concrete precipice, his body too, splashed under, at first, but then resurfaced. Shifting over, the would be lifeguard, brought into super-hero mode now, out of love instinct, took a deep breath, and swam under his daughter, hoping to push her up long enough for Marge to grab under a shoulder. With no handholds at all, edge of the reservoir side being rounded for better water flow, it was a struggle, and only on the third attempt did Marge lean back far enough and grasp long enough to haul the drenched little rat to safety.

"Daddy's a good swimmer, huh Mommy?" said Janey.

"Yes, Dear, Daddy's a very good swimmer."

"Can he swim better than the fish I saw, Mommy?" she asked, from the middle of a hug.

Superstan, himself still in deep, but mission accomplished, had to struggle some to haul his heavier than normal, from soaked clothes, body to the shore. He undressed to wring out his sweater, and jeans.

"Is Daddy draining the dragon over there, again?" asked Janey, herself naked now, for the same reason Daddy was.

"No, Daddy's just trying to get a bit drier, Dear."

Janey stared up at her Mother, oblivious to the danger, and unsure as to what had just occurred, asked, with obvious new excitement. "What about Daddy's monster fish, Mommy. Where is it?"

"It's still on the hook, Dear, Daddy will bring it in as soon as he gets dressed. We can watch him."

"I want to see it, Mommy. I want to see it."

"You'll see it, Dear, as soon as Daddy gets dressed, and reels it in."

"I saw it out there." Janey pointed her finger in the wrong direction, downstream, where she remembered the fish to be.

Meanwhile, over on the far shore, Stan had slithered out of clothes, had wrung them out as best he could, and faced another decision that only weird fishermen face. "Sorry about the delay, fishy boy, but you know, Superman's gotta do the right thing. Now it's your turn. Do you want to come out soon, or can you wait for Superman to redress?" This time his decision was not so obvious to Stan the fisherman, it being not life-death, and less urgent time wise. The longer he waited, the more chances old shark may have to get off the line, no? The clothes would still be there after he landed the fish, no? Marge and Janey were all right, no? His daughter was too far away to sight the Dragon, superhero's Dragon it had become, clearly, and his wife had seen it before, lots of times. So to heck with clothing. Let's just get that damned fish to shore, eh? Make the fisherman lineage proud.

So buck naked, the Dragon flopping fishlike, he strode over to the rod, pulled it out of the sand, and once again, after a ten minute delay of game penalty, started reeling.

"Why is Daddy naked?" asked Janey.

"I guess he really wants to make sure he catches the fish, Janey. Fish can get away if you leave them very long," replied Marge, with mixed feelings regarding her man over there fishing in the nude, momentarily. She understood his need to catch the fish, but also wished he'd put some clothes on first. She smiled, realizing perhaps he'd just saved Janey's life, so nude fishing, albeit weird, she'd tolerate, under this circumstance. No point saying anything, he'd already made up his mind, obviously.

The poor fish had exhausted itself during the delay. It came in like a weed. Stan lifted it up proudly beside his naked self for Janey to see, yelling, "Here is the fish, Janey. Do you see it?" It was a fine four pound specimen, for the Battle, meaty enough to feed the three of them, twice perhaps, if he didn't pig out.

Janey yelled back, "Yes, Daddy, I see it. It's a big fish." The fish captured her attention, so much that Daddy's nakedness was invisible.

The exhausted fisherman removed the sharp hook from the tired walleye's jaw, careful not to have it take a bite out of all the skin around, grabbed it's tail, walked calmly over to the edge of the Battle, gently released it, and whispered, "Can't eat you, Buddy. Not now. Superman doesn't eat fish, he just saves them. Off you go, and take care, the next fisherman might not be so kind."

# The Student Minister

The small rural church congregation needed ministering, and during the summers, as the congregation was unable to afford a full time minister, the national or provincial headquarters sent out a student minister to attend to the congregation's needs. Summer, for two months was ideal for both parties: the congregation, and the minister attending. Vacation Bible School occurred then, as the children were not preoccupied with regular school. A teen group just for the summer needed leadership. Families had fresh food to donate from their gardens, church picnics could happen regularly because of the weather, but most of all, the minister needed experience. Starting small at anything is best. A friendly rural down home community could be just the ticket to big time preacherhood. Getting a good review could mean an assistant minister's job in the future.

For the congregation, it was a time for rejoicing, a time when community could gather at the friendly local church instead of the unfamiliar one in town, and spiritual bonding in Love could occur. Renewed friendships, clean fun, and brotherhood. All this because, although it was temporary, at least it was a minister. Many not so regular members of the congregation were now able, or wanted, to attend, because the drive was about twenty miles less, and they recognized everybody. It wasn't just a bunch of strange townsfolk you didn't know. Every one there was a farmer, just like yourself. Indeed, the local folk looked forward to a summer of Sundays in church, even if old Marvin would snore, or Jane's kids would get bored and go outside only to poke their curious noses back into the window. This was family extended to community.

She arrived on a mission, heaven bent for success. Within two weeks, Gladys had dined with all the key members of the congregation, had begun a teen group that included fourteen members, not all of which were regulars, (but there was missionary conversion work), and was prepared for Vacation Bible School in three days. She was receiving nothing but praise by parishioners on how well she was fitting in. At the school picnic she had overheard many a "What a super student minister we have this year!" Little did she know that the parishioners judged their student ministers relatively, usually comparing the new one to the one from the previous summer, and he had been a real dud.

On a personal note, she had taken up with a dashing young man, Mr. Thomas Jackson, also relatively fresh to the community, a teacher in the rural school down the road. Tom had arrived the September before, and her coming was a welcome sight for him, as there was little opportunity for romance out here some twenty miles from town. Not too many singles clubs or dating services here. Exactly what he needed to spice up the summer, at least, and perhaps even more, if she was compatible.

The minister kept occupied at night with all her groups, so afternoon was the most suitable time for outings, of any kind, including romance. On the first introduction at the school's year end picnic, Tom suggested they spend some afternoons exploring, "I've had little chance to look about this region, and its sights. Since I'm off for the summer, perhaps you'd like to join me for drives. Together we can explore the community. People tell me there are a lot of scenic trails, especially down along the Battle River valley."

"Sounds like a good idea to me. Why don't you pick me up next Monday, right after lunch. I'll be at the church." She welcomed the chance, and the break from the church work, and something about the fellow's manner had impressed her.

On their first date/drive, he motored down the highway until a trail appearing to follow the river came into view. As he turned and drove along it, he remarked, "Gee, this *is* a pretty river valley. The folks were correct. I wonder how far this road goes?"

"Well, why don't you just drive along, and find out?" Gladys was the passenger, and had no more idea of where this whole thing would lead than he. The road, the relationship, the direction this circumstance was heading, was a substantial transition for her. Her world was being altered quickly. She had lived in a metro area all her life, and had spent two years in Bible school, where dating was supervised, or allowed only in the company of friends. Weekends and holidays to this point in her life, had been with family. She welcomed the opportunity for independence, and the possibilities of new life-enriching experience that accompanied it. Besides, it was time she found out who she was. It was the sixties and part of her was drawn to the freedom ideas that she had only read about in church literature, and much of that had been critical. She was not so sure. Much of what the drug culture hippy generation was saying appeared right on to her, although she dared not express it, or worse, act on it, for fear of being banished from the program. Out here she felt safer. The elders were her new congregation, and they were all preoccupied with the business of survival, by farming, so she didn't feel as watched, at least not during the afternoons.

He was an American transplant, having lived in Seattle, and had come to Canada because teaching positions were not just available, and paid better than in the States. Besides, there was still the possibility of him being drafted, and shipped off to Nam, to perhaps die a horrible death, or worse become permanently dismembered, at the hands of the Viet Cong. Sure, Canada was cold, but cold was nothing compared to mosquito infested jungles where people who you didn't necessarily disagree with anyway, would take well aimed shots at you. Besides, the school board here provided him with a teacherage, and at least it was warm, and a short walk over to the school. What he had not anticipated was the loneliness. His only other adult friends had been the two other teachers. To some extent, his students had become his friends. There was no outlook or outlet for romance. When *she* arrived, it was a godsend, although he was not really into God. Adventure and free spirit were what drove him, in accepting this teaching position. The community suspected it, if only in a mildly connotative way from their reading of the peace revolts, because his vehicle was a tiny yellow Volkswagen.

She fell for the Volkswagen. It gave her a sense of rebellion, and although she knew it wouldn't go over well with her traditional parents, she could always say, "Well, that was *his* car. What could I do?" Besides, who would know, if she didn't tell? Her motive in this new beginning was all exploration: of world, of relationship, of nature, of herself. It was if she had been sent by the mission to a foreign country. A whopping cultural change.

Tom's motive was different than hers. He wanted some action, and figured if he played his cards right, he might just get it. Sure, if she turned out to be compatible in personality, that might be fine. He doubted that it would, given her background in church, and his not in church. He attended her first sermon mostly as a front. Not really to listen. Yet, there was truth, at least brotherhood, here, in church, he could tell, if not for him, at least for the devotees of the community. Why else would they all be smiling?

His background, however, had been different than hers. At college, he had, on the fringe, at least, partaken of much of the free love generation's rebellion. He'd bought the Volkswagen then, and had experimented with marijuana, LSD, and free love, if only on weekends. Teacher college had held his attention Mondays through Fridays, enough for him to at least pass, and had gotten him out of the war. In some ways he had grown to regret the move to rural Alberta. There was nothing resembling free love here, and he missed it. He had been able to afford only one trip back to Seattle, at Christmas time, and although he made the most of that, it was nowhere near enough to satisfy his needs.

At the time, he had no one to brag to of his week back home, although when his students politely asked, "How was your holiday in Seattle, Mr. Jackson?", he had to lie that it was the long drive that had him looking this way, not the week of unabashed partying, or three straight nights of smoking dope, or the one nighter of free love with Jane.

He'd wished that he could have found a job in a city, where he could have had much more opportunity to act on his sexual needs, or partying needs, and not been subject to any scrutiny by community. His total partying all year since Christmas had been Friday or Saturday smoke dope sessions by himself in front of a TV at the teacherage, and the dope he had brought back from Seattle had run out in May. Whatever, today was today, and he was up to making the most of it.

The Sampson sisters, Becky and Anne were bored. It was another week until Vacation Bible school started, and the adventures of summer beckoned out to them. Mom was always busy in the garden, or milking cows, or cooking, while Dad was always on the tractor in the fields, or fixing some machine or another. Thank God they had bicycles. The one thing they had to look forward to besides the day-long bicycle trips was the new student minister, Miss Davis. They had met her at the school picnic, and she was a beaut, both in looks, and personality. Mom had introduced them, "Girls, I'd like you to meet Miss Davis. She's the new student minister.

Miss Davis had asked, "Are you two coming to Bible school?"

"Yes, of course. We'll be there for sure. We've never missed it." That was all Becky had been able to say, as everyone had been eager to meet the new minister. Becky and Anne, along with the other girls in the grade 5/6 class, had giggled when their teacher, Mr. Jackson, had been introduced to her. The girls knew the marital status of each, and whenever the chance of a new romance was struck up, the appropriate response from young girls was giggling. In part, they envied Miss Davis, as she was older than they, and could act on her desire, if she had any. Yet, they realized that they too would have ample opportunity to rope and capture young men, only they would have to wait a few more years, until age brought independence.

Anne had rolled her eyes, "I wish I was her." The crush on Teach had lasted all year, and now he was gone - at least she was gorgeous, good enough for him, lucky guy.

The very first Monday, having listened to Miss Davis's inspired sermon about getting on with life, and revelling God's creative genius to be found in Mother nature, the pair asked Mom if they could pack a picnic, and explore the Battle valley, some three miles away. Mom had been a bit hesitant to grant permission, yet she too had been inspired by Miss Davis. If you can't enjoy nature when you're young, you might not be able to when you're older, when loaded with responsibility, such as she was. Might as well let them go. The worst that could happen was a flat tire, and even then they could walk home. "Be back by suppertime, okay. And don't go swimming in the river. Your father will take you down some evening."

The girls set out about nine, with a neat lunch they had prepared themselves tied in the basket of Anne's bike. They headed down to the river, and had planned a circular route along the old trail on their home side, a total distance of about fifteen miles, which would be easy and relaxing. Perhaps they might see wildlife. At worst, they were sure to get exercise, coming back up the steep hill, where they knew the bikes would have to be pushed. By ten, they had reached the trail. Such scenery. Scenery they had never enjoyed until now, thanks to Miss Davis's inspiring fresh view of this part of their world.

Thomas spoke of freedom, too. "You know, Gladys, I really enjoyed your sermon yesterday. It made me see things differently about these parts. I always thought these folks were a bit stuck in their ways, but yesterday at church, you seemed to be able to pull the best cheer out of them, especially when you talked of the beauty of God's creation. I think I've been missing it a bit. In Seattle I used to go down to the ocean beach, and just smell the fresh air. It was a lot different than here, but your sermon illustrated that God's creation is everywhere, even here on the prairies, where there is little to look at. Take this valley, for instance. It's a perfect example of what you said." He was complimenting, and sucking up, at once.

"Yes, I know. On the way here, I drove through the valley two or three times. There aren't many glacial valleys in the city. You just don't appreciate this sort of thing there. Here it seems special. It's so isolated from the farms above, and you get the sense almost that we're the only ones on the planet."

"Perhaps we are." Tom stopped the Bug at a bend in the road. "Let's go for a walk over to the river. I'm sure this road won't go on forever."

Gladys agreed. "That's good. I need fresh air. Your car smells a bit of gas, anyway."

"It's just that it burns a little oil. I bought this thing in Seattle, and I can't seem to dish it, because I'm attached. It has too many good memories in it. The heater doesn't work well. Last winter I only drove it once a week to go to town for groceries." The conversation was coming along.

"I hate driving. I'm glad you enjoy it. This is the first time I've ever ridden in a Volkswagen. I like it."

The young couple were getting along, perhaps because of the similar bond of feeling outcast, in the ruralness of the place. This they shared. She asked him to tell her of the people he had met so far.

"Well, I haven't had any problems with them. For the most part, they are very traditional people. All farmers. The ones you meet will be mostly religious, and will have strong moral obligations like working hard, and taking Sundays off. Although last fall during harvest time, and this spring, I saw them out on Sundays. Last fall many of my students, mostly the boys, had poor attendance, because of harvest. I got used to having half a class, for about three weeks. The kids here are strong, and all work hard at school. I don't know the adults well, except that they all supported whatever I did at school. Tell me something about you."

Gladys felt obliged to share something of herself, "Well, as you can tell, I'm religious. I guess that goes without saying. My parents always kept a pretty strong rope on me. This is about the first time I've ever been alone with a man. I'm looking forward to getting out and about more. I'd never even been to a movie, until after high school. I don't really regret it, but I wish we could have travelled more when I was younger. This is about as far as I've ever been outside of Edmonton."

"So how come you decided to become a minister?" Thomas wanted to know just how puritan thinking she was.

"Well, mostly my parents encouraged me a lot. Sometimes through the church, they'll send you overseas. It's an opportunity to travel, without feeling unsafe. Maybe next year I can get a missionary job in Africa, for instance. It's exciting. But of course, you have to prove yourself. So that's why I'm here. Do you know the Sampson family at all?"

"Yes. The younger sister was in my class, in fact. I got to know the mother as well as anyone, I suppose. She's pretty sane. Never gave me any trouble. The other teacher told me she really likes compliments, especially about her daughters, so I said a lot of good things about Anne to her. No complaints."

"Well, she's on the board. At the end of my eight weeks out here, they have to fill in a report on me, which will be filed in church headquarters. I'd like to please them." Gladys wanted some advice, if Tom had any.

"Well, all you have to do is keep telling her how nice her daughters are, but don't make it obvious, that that's what you're doing. Besides, the daughter's *are* really nice, so it won't be hard finding compliments."

The couple struggled to get through about twenty yards of heavy underbrush, before coming out upon the river, where there was a sandy stepped edge that showed various levels of flow through the year. The river curved sharply, and had a steep bank on the opposite shore. They spotted a couple of flat rocks solid enough to sit on to dangle feet in the water. As they approached, Tom picked up a small flat stone, and skipped it in one hop across the river. Together they took shoes and socks off, he curling up his pantlegs, and she hitching up her dress a bit, placed the shoes neatly in the grass, and sat, all twenty toes in the stream.

"Wow, you must have played ball," she said, referring to his stone skipping.

"Just when I was a kid. I coached here. These kids were pretty good, considering everyone had to play. Back when I grew up, only the richer of us and the better athletes got to play. Here, if all the kids didn't play, you wouldn't have a team."

"You enjoyed that?" she asked.

"Yup. We went to town, and beat the team from town. Now that the kids really enjoyed, because they knew that the town kids had a lot more athletes from which to draw from." He was part bragging, part telling. "Do you play ball?"

"No. I never had the chance. I can throw a bit." She picked up a rock, tossed it from her sitting position, and it didn't skip, but plunked about ten yards out in the water.

"That's not bad. If you want to make it skip, you need the right rock, and you have to throw it with a bit more force, at an angle that's close to the water." He got back up, found another rock, and demonstrated, again.

She was not overly impressed. "It doesn't matter. Come and sit down. I just want to talk. When you were young playing ball, were you one of the rich kids, or one of the good athletes?"

"I was one of the rich kids, I guess. Not really rich. Just middle class. But I would have rather been one of the good athletes." He was honest.

"Why?"

"Because money doesn't count in those situations after awhile. Once you hit about sixteen, if you don't have the talent, you can't continue in sports. I had to quit. There were no teams for the ungifted."

"Okay, so then what did you do with your time?" she inquired.

"Well in the States, they have this ugly thing they call the draft, and a war, you know. My parents couldn't fathom me over there getting shot at. Neither could I, so I took teacher training, and applied for a job up here in Canada where it's safer. That's pretty much why I'm here."

"Well, I for one, am glad you are. I have company." She sounded content.

"How deep do you think the water is out there?" he asked. He had to get after this some time. Might as well get it over with. If she didn't follow this train, he'd stop."

"I bet it's over your head,"she answered. She was not at all suspicious of where this conversation could lead.

Becky and Anne stopped at the bridge on the main road. The trail they were destined for was on their side, but the bridge was a place to explore. They parked the bikes in the ditch, and ventured out onto the wooden planks that crossed the one lane metal structure.

Anne looked down into the river. "I think the river is low for this time of the year. What do you think, Beck?"

"I never notice it one way or another. We just drive right on over it usually. Remember?" Becky questioned her little sister, because it seemed odd that Anne would notice such things.

"I was just kind of pondering Miss Davis's words from yesterday. She said we would all be happier if we noticed nature more. I was noticing. Is that okay?" Anne replied.

"Of course that's okay. I think it's good that you're noticing. Come to think of it, this little river is remarkable. Do you ever wonder where it goes to?" Becky too was adhering to the more philosophical flow begun yesterday.

"I think it goes to Saskatchewan. In fact I know it does." Anne expressed her geography knowledge.

"Yeah, I know. I think we learned that in grade four. But actually being here is so different than reading it in a textbook or looking at a map. Funny, here we are on holidays, and we're talking school."

"I wonder how long it takes for the water molecules here to travel to Saskatchewan," Anne conjectured.

"Well, you know what we should do next time. We should put a note in a bottle or in two bottles, you know, like they do in stories, and then toss the bottles over, and wait. One day maybe someone could pick it up, and we'd get a story." A plan for a later day summer activity had begun.

"Well, we'd have to decide what all to put in it. We'd have to find a good bottle," Anne continued.

This gave Becky a large-scale idea. "Well, what we should do is suggest this to Miss Davis next week at Vacation School. Maybe we could all ride down here, and throw a whole bunch of bottles in together."

"It could be a contest," added Anne.

"Yes, and we could get Mother to offer up a prize for the furthest travelled or something like that." Becky knew Mom could be convinced of almost anything, when it had to do with church.

"I like it!" said Anne.

"We'd need tough bottles." Becky, although the idea sounded grand, realized details needed to be thought out. It'd be better in the spring when water flow is up."

"Probably no one would find any."

"You'd never know until you try. That's what Dad is always saying."

The girls continued to plan this bottle in river fantastic idea as they rode casually along the trail downstream from the bridge.

"Well, I bet you I can walk right across without having to swim." Tom was liking this bet, and the conversation turn, more and more.

"But it's such a steep bank on the other side. The water looks deep from here. If the water follows the curvature of the other bank, it's probably way over your head near the other side." Gladys found the hypothetical situation interesting. It was almost spiritual to her, as the unknown, such as death, was. "If you can't see it, you can't tell how deep it is."

Tom explained. "In the ocean, in a boat, sometimes you can see the bottom, but even then it's deceptive. Sometimes from the boat it looks like a few feet, but then when you jump in, it's ten feet or so. Depends a lot on the current, and the weather, and stuff. Here it's hard to tell.

"Well, I guess we'll never know. We don't have a boat, and measuring the depth in current must be hard anyway. An anchor wouldn't work because it would be at an angle." Gladys seemed satisfied at letting the mystery be. There were lots of things in life that one would never know, at least without action, such as chopping down a tree in order to determine it's age.

Tom sensed that she was ready for a change of topic, so purposefully continued with this one. "Well, there is one way to find out. I could just go for a swim right out there, and see if I could walk across or not."

She looked surprised. "You wouldn't?"

"Why not?" he shot back.

"Well, you'd get all wet," she explained, "and have to make your car stink up even more."

Determined, he continued, "People tell me they swim in this river all the time. I'll take my clothes off. They'll stay dry."

"You wouldn't?" This time she was more surprised, and stared at him.

"Well, I don't see why not. In Seattle, I used to go swimming in the ocean at the nude beach all the time."

"You mean you're going in nude? Aren't you going to at least leave your underwear on?" Now she was questioning directly, not just him, but her whole minister/ethical upbringing. What was she doing here, with this almost total stranger, in the middle of nowhere. "What if someone comes along?" she asked, hoping he would reconsider, out of fear.

"The trail was almost never travelled. I don't see anyone around. Seems like a very secluded spot. All the farmers are busy in their fields. Besides, we would hear any cars coming along."

"That could be, but I'm still against it. It's not religion like."

He continued, not forcefully, but softly, intellectually, "Look, we were born nude. It's natural. In yesterday's sermon, wasn't it you that was going on and on about appreciating Mother Nature more."

She couldn't disagree on this. "Well, yes, I guess I was. But I was referring more to trees, and animals, and scenery, not human nudity."

"So you're saying that humans are not natural?"

"No, not that. It's just that you know, it's not very common. Maybe I'm just not quite ready for this," she answered, knowing that he was making some sense, but afraid of the possibility of her entering a different realm.

He stared at her. "How old are you, Gladys?"

"I'm twenty-one. How old are you, by the way?" She was becoming a little more relaxed.

"I'm twenty-three, just two years older than you. Don't you think that you're an adult?"

Reluctant to admit it, she left some doubt in her response. "Well, yes, I *guess* I am."

"Well, adults wouldn't really have a big problem with this." He stood up, and started undoing his shirt.

"Well, I'm certainly not watching you. You can just tell me how deep the river is. She turned away. He stripped, bare to the bone. Thomas had been swimming nude many times with friends back in Seattle so this was no big deal to him. This wasn't even the first time he'd done it in the company of a female companion.

She continued looking the other way. "Yell to me when you're in over your head. No, not that, that's not what I mean. I mean over your... well, you know what I mean. Decent." She blushed.

"You mean I'm not decent now?" He was forward.

"Oh, you're a decent enough person, at least that's what I think. You know what I mean. Just hurry up and get in the water."

"Okay." Tom waded in, yelping at first, "It's a bit chilly," and then continued until he was up to his chest, which was still not across the river. At that point he called back. "Okay, I'm in far enough for you to turn around."

She turned and looked at the top half of a man she didn't know that well. "So how deep is it?" she half called, half talked, as still she expected someone might hear her, even way down here. No use taking chances. As if the chance bit hadn't already gone too far.

"I can't tell. I'll just keep backing up." Slowly he backed up. "The water is really warm once you get used to it. I think that the bottom is leveling off a bit.

Soon he was up to his neck, but he could feel the bottom leveling off, and within another yard, coming back up. "Well, that's about it. I can tell it's getting shallow again. I'm starting to go back up. I guess I win the bet."

Back about a mile upstream, Becky and Anne had stopped again, along a lookout point about ten metres higher than the river bed. "I think I can see some sort of bird out there in the middle of the river, Becky."

"Point to where you see it," Becky requested.

Anne did as she was told. "It's a tall thing right there in the middle on that island."

Becky, too, spotted it. "Wow, look at that. It must be after fish. At least minnows."

"Do you have any idea what it is, Becky?" Anne wanted more knowledge today.

"Well, I've heard that there are big birds called herons that live in places like this. Only I don't know if they live here or not. If I remember right, the book said eastern and southern Canada," Becky shared whatever wisdom she had.

"Well, this is Canada." Anne affirmed.

Becky looked at her sister stupidly, "Yes, Anne, I know."

"So then it's a heron."

"Yes, a great grey or great blue heron. Some color anyway." Becky was a bit unsure still, having to jog her own memory of science.

"Neat. This place is neat. I never knew we could see so much on a simple trip so close to home. I can't wait to tell Mom everything we've seen. I bet you she doesn't even know half this stuff." This was Anne's first mention of going home, and sharing. It certainly was more exciting than the stuff they had learned the last ten months. "Becky, don't you think it's weird that we are learning more out here than we did at school. At least it seems that way to me."

"Yes, Sis, I agree. There is a lot of difference between seeing a bird and just reading about one, isn't there?"

Gladys was not going to give in so easily on the bet. "Well, I'm not so sure if you win the bet. Just because at that particular spot, you can cross, doesn't mean that if you swam two or three yards further upstream, or downstream, it wouldn't be over your head."

Tom called back, "Then I'll just have to swim upstream a bit, and check it out. That's easy. If I can't touch bottom, you'll know, because my head will go under." He pushed off the bottom, and flung one arm, then the other, to swim a few feet upstream. "Tell me when you want me to stop."

"Right there," she yelled out. "Try it right there."

Tom straightened up, and gently let himself sink. She was right. It was over his head. He sunk below the surface to the point where the water level was at his elbow, with arm extended. Then he resurfaced, and called out, "So now how are we going to tell who was right?"

"I'd be happy to call it a tie. It depends on exactly where we were pointing when you were over here on shore, doesn't it, and we could discuss that all day," she predicted.

"You're absolutely right, Gladys. There's no point. You know, the water's really warm. Why don't you join me for a swim? It'll cool you down in this hot weather." He was prepared to take a shot. Now that she hadn't insisted that he drive her home, when he decided to go for a dip, perhaps just maybe she'd join him. He had little to lose.

She did not respond. She just looked at him, and shrugged her shoulders. Her whole conflict in life passed over her. An image of her mother sort of appeared between her ears, saying, "Now, Gladys, you know that you must follow the Lord, and his commandments." She reflected. Time, God, how she wished she had some more of it. She would be gone in another six weeks. So would this opportunity. Would this be one of her few lifetime chances at romance?

Tom could not tell the reason for all the silence, so he broke it, "You know, in lots of places, this is normal. In Seattle, groups of us went skinny-dipping all the time. It's nature's way. It's not like we're going to make love or anything. Like I said, the water is really warm, and it feels good all over. A lot more refreshing than anything else you can do. Out in this fresh clean air. This water is a lot better than the salt water of the ocean, too."

"Okay." She was still not sure. "You're sure about that?"

"Look, Gladys, if you don't want to come in, don't. That's fine by me. You wouldn't be doing this for me. You would be doing it for you. Life is meant to be lived, no? This could very well be your only chance in life to live a little. Unless you get a posting somewhere where you have a lot of room for self expression, my guess is it won't happen." He was half true to himself in his convincing. Although he had other motives, he knew they could come later.

"Okay, I'm doing it." The half real image of her mother, standing there in front of her, preaching goodness, and purity, but not always practicing it, was the final card that won her over to his side. All the restrictions of childhood, of the church, and of her own self-imposed discipline fell by the wayside. He was right. She could see no real wrong in this, other than mischief. Besides, he was out there having fun in rebellion, and she was sitting here, on this rock, feeling blue from life's impending stability. She stood up, reached down to grab the bottom of her dress, and pulled it up over her head, revealing her modest panties, and bra, which too had been selected by mother, and reminded her once more of that dependence she held.

"You won't regret this, Gladys." Tom proudly beamed, in admiration, both for his winning her over, and for this girl's new found rebellious nature, that he had only catalysed.

The sisters continued along the trail. Anne spotted it first, as they rounded a corner in the trail, "Look, Becky, there's a car up ahead."

"It looks like Mr. Jackson's car," Becky observed.

"Yup, it sure does. I wonder what he's doing down here." Anne questioned, as she knew that school was out, and wondered why Mr. Jackson hadn't gone back to Seattle, like he had said he was going to, when she'd asked him, the last week of school.

"Maybe it's not his car, Anne." Becky added. "There are other yellow Volkswagens in the world, you know."

"Well, I haven't seen any around here. I bet it is his." Anne was convinced, confident of her own statistical ability.

"You're probably right. We'll find out when we get there, eh?" Becky sped ahead, with Anne close to follow.

Anne called ahead. "Becky, I think we should sneak up on him and surprise him. That would be fun."

At this suggestion, Becky slowed her pace to give Anne a chance to catch up. "Yes, that would be fun."

Gladys Davis, soon to be full fledged ordained minister, was wading into a small unknown river, in the middle of nowhere, on the 2nd of July, 1969, in full frontal view of a man she hardly knew, who drove a Volkswagen, and talked a lot. If Mommy could only see her little pig-tailed girl now. Gladys shook her head as the water level hit her knees, "I can't believe you talked me into this." The shaking of head was soon overcome by the quirky smile on her face. Freedom, at last. There was no turning back.

Soon the girls were at the car. "I told you this was his." Becky reiterated her initial observation. They stopped, and listened.

"I hear voices," whispered Anne, "Sounds like from over by the river."

They gently set the bikes down in the grass beside the VW. "Let's sneak through the bushes, and surprise them." suggested Becky. She knew from experience the pair could sneak through bushes. They'd done it before, around home, lots of times.

Slowly, watching every step for dead branches, they snuck, as if they were tropical native hunters sneaking up on deer in the jungle. Neither spoke. Both heard the two voices. Eventually Anne could not resist the sharing of her voice recognition skills, "Becky, she whispered, "it sounds like Miss Davis is here, too."

"That's good. We can surprise them both. But we have to be really quiet." Becky put her forefinger to her lips to gesture silence.

After about ten minutes of sneaking, they arrived to a point behind a large Russian poplar that would enable a view of the river ahead. Becky let Anne put her head around the tree, which was wider than both of them together. After about five seconds, of jaw agape staring, Anne turned, and gestured total total silence, pointing back in the general direction of the road, saying, with her finger, "Let's get out of here!"

Becky could not figure out the body language for sure, so had to have a peek for herself. Her suspicions were confirmed when she saw the Adam and Eve figures moving about in the waste deep water, splashing each other, reminding her more of farm kittens playing about, than of a school teacher, and Sunday school teacher. Only thing was that this Adam had no fig leaf, and she had never seen a totally bare mature female either. She turned and nodded to her little sister in agreement of the, "Let's get out of here!"

Back on the road, they jumped on their bikes, and wheeled it, not stopping, or slowing, for at least a mile. Each mind racedover the possible scenarios that would could come of this adventure. Telling Mom would mean losing Miss Davis for the summer, and the probable cancellation of Vacation School. Mr. Jackson may lose his teaching job. Both adults would certainly have confrontations to deal with. Finally, Becky pulled over to rest, and talk, having already made up her mind of what to do.

"Anne, we can't tell anyone. I like Miss Davis, and Mr. Jackson. We'll ruin them if we tell anyone. Don't tell anyone, okay."

"Becky, you stole my thoughts." Anne, too, had thought it through.

"Promise?"

"Promise."

# Daniel S. Perkins - The First Sale

No one had ever heard what the S stood for, but it served him well, becoming the initial of his nickname, Swampy, in years to follow. People claimed the name was for the muskeggy area where he had set up shop along the river, on a flat feeder spring below the hills, and for his hairy unkept appearance, and smell, although no one ever mentioned those two reasons to his face, preferring to use the muskeg excuse. Most people were just too polite. "He's named that because he lives in a swamp patch," fathers replied to inquisitive children. Truth was he earned the tag from the store owner in town, when he came in looking and smelling the way he did. He himself never ever knew of the nickname. Other people just called him Perkins, or Mr. Perkins.

Initially, he had been awed by the beauty of the isolated place. (Isolation was agreeable to the neighbours, too.) Nothing but pioneer optimism had enveloped his soul as he had chosen the quarter to homestead, down in the valley, where he could ranch, and do less fencing, as the Battle would provide a natural barrier for the cows. It reminded him of home in the Catskills, where he'd grown up, but had left for the spirit of adventure and freedom's call had possessed him. Besides, Ma and Pa treated him like the runt of the litter, never giving much and expecting lots back, in the way of labor, which he disdained, as he was a lazy, sloppy guy by nature.

But, to his discouragement, small time ranching had been largely unproductive in the river valley, not to mention the having to work hard part. He had grossly underestimated the wandering ability of cattle. Back home they had log fences that worked. It seemed those cattle were always getting off of his quarter, or as he inaccuratelty imagined, were rustled by the unscrupulous folks down the way. If the truth be known, he was just a lousy fencer, and the Battle was a pathetic boundary. Sure, the future had looked good when he'd started, but after a few drought years, the runaway cattle made him broke, a beggar, out here by himself, in the midst of naught but scenic views, which didn't put much grub on the table. To survive, he either had to depart, or to come up with a new creative scheme. He was against moving on, as this place did have its natural strengths, like the river, and he had managed to eek out survival for now. It was just a simple matter of picking up a bit more cash for his twice a year trips to town for basics, like flour, and matches. Dreamy laziness had lead to the original plan, and dreamy laziness lead to this one.

When prohibition came along, it soon occurred to him that there was an old familiar product, that was about to take a sharp upswing in market value, and that he held some expertise in the field. Lots of folks had dropped by on their way across the Battle between two developed rail lines, and had partaken of his rhubarb stew, as he liked to call it, after the primary mash ingredient, before the fermentation. Rhubarb was a lot quicker than some of the other grainy kinds, because it had more sugar. It hadn't been a product, really, more just a hobby, like growing your own vegetables. He only fired the thing up once a year, in the fall, when the rhubarb plants gave their finest displays of foliage, and had never run out, although lately with all his other troubles, it had been close. Moonshine served the purpose of relaxing him, and welcoming any guest who would partake, normally other ranchers on horseback out looking for a stray, or the real men of real families moving in.

He'd remembered the compliments of many a real man who now dwelt on the flats above:

"Boy, this is tasty stew."

"A lot better than the stuff they serve in town."

"Goes down smooth. Packs a good wallop, though."

"Can I have another shot?"

"Where'd you learn to make this stuff?"

"You can't even get it legally now, you know. Stupid government made it illegal."

"Geez, Swampy, what are ya ranching for?"

The last one stuck in his head, especially now, with the prohibition. So he decided to take a break from ranching, a semi-retirement, and set up primarily in the moonshine biz, which for sure he had more skill at. There'd even be less work, after the initial season, and the idea of sitting around more, chasing damn cows less, intrigued him. Oh, he'd keep a few cows, for they made a good cover should the mounties ever get wind. Besides, he was a rancher first, albeit not a very skilled one, and liked cattle around, especially the tamer ones. A few head would suffice. And it would take him a year or so, to get really established.

There were things to do before a real quality product could be produced in any quantity. Remembering back to his childhood, he recalled that the true blue shiners, the guys who made a business of it, always tested the product on a willing guinea pig first, and in their case the guinea pig was a real pig. If the pig dropped over in its own muck, this batch was most likely unfit for humans. He'd never bothered with such elaboration before, figuring he could test it himself by taking small swigs. But now, if business boomed, and he figured it would, he'd need a quicker more solid testing method. One where you can take a darn good slug all at once, and not worry about it burning your guts, or permanently damaging your eyes. He didn't have any hogs, being as he hated the smell of them so much. Not like cattle or horses. "No point smelling up this valley with those darn things," he'd told himself. But they'd be excellent testers, cheaper, and not like cows. Closer in constitution to humans anyway. Closer to him in smell, too, but he wasn't aware, just as someone with bad breath can't tell.

So with his change of career plan, he rode Lizzy, his mare, the best female company he ever had, up to the flats to the nearest place that owned any bacon. The McMillans had pigs, but were somewhat of a Christian Bible punching lot, although he'd seen worse, and Ed McMillan had refused the offer of some rhubarb stew the only time he'd been inside Swampy's place. So Swampman figured he'd bend the reason a tad, if McMillan were to question.

"Hi, there, Perkins. What can I do for you?" Ed McMillan inquired, this being the only time the somewhat of a hermit in the valley had ever stopped this way.

Swampy explained why he'd come. "I need to get me a couple of hogs. Want to change my setup a bit. Damn cows keep running off on me somewheres. I figured you might have a couple I could trade for."

McMillan questioned further, knowing Swampy wouldn't have any cash, and had few belongings he wouldn't need. "Just what are you offering?"

"Well, I figured I could give you a couple of my yearling heifers, if you could give me a few of those pigs."

"Well, I don't know, Mr. Perkins. Those heifers of yours are pretty wild from what I hear." McMillan wasn't about to lose at bartering, nor did he want wild cattle to infiltrate his small herd. He just wanted a fair deal, and figured although he held sympathy for Swampy, still it'd be the Lord's way to be just. He stood and waited for Swampy to re offer.

"What are you thinking?" Swampy stared in befuddlement at the silent neighbour. Swampy wasn't used to conversation, and often misunderstood. "Do you have any pigs you could spare, or not? If not, I'll just go on down the road til I find a man who does. Just came here cause it was the closest place."

"Well, then, there isn't much case you going any further. We have three or four you could have. You gonna start raising them?" McMillan needed to know so he could provide the poor guy with some right start up advice. Maybe Swampy just needed one, for devouring purposes, come winter.

"Well, just a few, you know. I'm not gonna switch over completely. First I gotta build me a pen, I guess. That'll take a while." Whenever Swampy said 'a while', it meant quite a lot longer than the normal person's 'while'.

McMillan knew now that Swampy was going to begin raising them, and figured in this case 'while' meant about a month. "Tell you what, Swampy, when you get it all ready, bring two of your best heifers up here, and sure, we can trade. You can have your pick of any five young piglets. That ought to get you started. Later you can add to your bunch from somewhere else. That's the best way."

"Sounds like a good deal to me," replied Swampy, not realizing or caring if he'd done okay in the bartering process. Besides, soon enough his desirable fresh product would be in. Next fall, in fact. Maybe sooner. He extended his hand, the two shook on it, and Swampy hopped back on Lizzy and rode back down the hill home, happier than a pig in manure, and just as filthy, as always.

Swampy had one more resource to build up, before he could fire up the still more often, and that was his rhubarb crop. Until now, he had only needed about four plants. The swamp he lived on was ideal, superb soil, a bit sandy, and wet, very. Moisture from the river soaked up through the soil, and rhubarb shot up like sunflowers. The tropics for three months. He hadn't bothered to help it spread at all, but now there was a valid reason, so he split each plant up by the roots into fours, and moved it about, hoping each new plant would flourish. Flourish it did.

Rhubarb was such a versatile plant that Swampy wondered why people hadn't found even more uses for it. Besides the stew use, Swampy liked to smoke it. All you had to do was set the leaves out to dry, and if your timing was on, you could roll it up, like cigars. The old hermit, damn near self sufficient completely, often wondered why other people went to the hassle of importing tobacco from the east. Rhubarb leaves even tasted better, and if they got too dry, you just used the pipe. He'd shared this product with some stoppers by as well, but it didn't seem to turn them on the way the stew did. Maybe if times got real tough, he could market that, too.

All that summer Swampy worked harder than any summer before. More sweat than on just hot days, which kept the old goat cleaner, as he headed for the river to cool down, little realizing that his cool downs also were baths, much to the relief of anyone who stopped. He more or less gave up on 'those damn cows' and concentrated every effort into producing an extensive rhubarb plantation, even hauling water by hand up the hundred yards or so from the river to nourish them. He pulled down some of the cattle fencing, and built a pen for the pigs, one that would serve the purpose, just barely.

Fortunately, not all of the cows wandered too far from his earlier haphazard fencing, and in late summer, he managed to herd two heifers up to McMillans to exchange for the pigs. He figured he'd butcher one of them that year, and use the rest as guinea pigs, over time. This was a helluva deal! Getting rid of those wild creatures. What McMillan didn't know wouldn't hurt him. So what for the smell. Besides, these critters seemed simpler to herd, because they followed him along, when he walked alongside Lizzy, instead of the other way around, the way of cattle. Truth was the piglets figured he was one of them, perhaps their mother, and were duped. Upcoming cash would compensate for the smell, and the work. Next year he could use their manure to bolster the growth of rhubarb even more. Gee, in five years, he figured he could go back to just making enough for his own use. Besides, he put the pig pen to the east of his shack, where unwanted odors could waff down the valley.

He rode the thirty miles into town, twice, and managed to scrounge around in the garbage dump for some empty brown glass bottles, which were readily available now, because of the prohibition, and took them to his factory by the river. He scrubbed them up using fresh river water, which wasn't always terribly sanitary. Might as well sell a clean product, he reasoned. Fortunately for the potential customers, his rhubarb stew itself massacred any bacteria, and dissolved any grit he may not have noticed through the side of the brown bottles.

By the middle of September he was absolutely prepared. Bottles, water, lots of ready firewood from all the dead wood lying around his place and up on the slopes, if necessary, and most crucial of all, the best rhubarb crop he'd had, in the fifteen years since arriving. It was time to fire up the mini-distillery. Swampy had been anticipating this day all summer.

He moved it a quarter mile up to a draw, and set up a temporary shelter, twice the size of an outhouse, and hauled several huge armfuls of the precious rhubarb, throwing it into the largest vat he had, and set to boiling it up, to make the mushy goo, and let it simmer until it rotted, then let the rig do it's own work, with him attending to the small fire needed just to keep it steaming.

Within a week, he had a cupful of the potent stuff, and treated the cup with the sacredness of a dying monk making his final offering to an icon. He carried it down to the pigpen, and called one of the young hogs over. He had been treating them to rhubarb since they'd arrived, as a treat from the other native plants which were there usual fodder, and figured this stuff would have enough rhubarb flavor to entice them. The hogs had grown to like his company, as he spent lots of time in their midst, inside the pen. He grabbed the closest one, the one with one browner spot, whom he had named Larry, by the neck, and sat down beside it in the muck, with the trial cup in hand. At first he just held it out to the guinea, but young Larry seemed wary of the stuff, so he held on to Larry's head better, leaned it back, and poured the whole half cup of sauce down the animal's throat. Larry nearly choked, but then started licking inside it's mouth to indicate the taste had agreed with him. Swampy released it, and retreated to the edge of the pen, just to watch the outcome.

The stuff had effect within about five minutes, and Larry came hustling right over to Swampy, and started tail-wagging like an amorous dog, but it's tail wasn't there, just its behind was. It looked up at Swampy with eyes aglare as if to say, "Give me more. It was darn tasty." Then Larry, the now liquored-happy creature, went a cruising after it's playmates, the other hogs, and caused them to respond to his friendly gestures. By this time, Swampy knew for sure his stuff was pure, but he stayed awhile just to watch the action. Larry bounced around with his pigsiblings, rolled in the muck, tasted some of it, regurgitating most, and had a couple of unsuccessful attempts at leaping over the fence, while every few seconds looking over at Swampy, the audience, to get applause for the show. Eventually he tired of the action, and flopped on his back right in the middle of the pen, not caring where he was, eyes watching clouds, looking for pig shapes in them, and dozed off, all four feet pointed skywards, and ripping huge snores that startled the other hogs, including Swampy.

Swampy returned to work, cup in hand, satisfied the test was over, and figuring that Larry would be willing to go for it again with the next batch. He wore a path between home and factory over the next three weeks, and by Thanksgiving, had the first few bottles collected, and corked, raring to take up to a Thanksgiving dance some ten miles beyond the curve of the hill, where the ranchers met with the farmers to celebrate the season's success, or in some years, their collective mere survival. McMillan had told him about it one day in passing, when he'd stopped to check out Swampy's new setup

The day of the opening sale finally arrived, and the former rancher, now distiller, wrapped the ten bottles of prime shaker in, what else, rhubarb leaves, to protect the darlings from breaking, put them in a gunny sack, and headed up to the community hall where his unknowing customers were surely eager to partake of divinity itself. It seemed to him that Lizzy too sensed something special, for it was rare indeed that she was saddled in the evening.

About a mile from his market, he had a bit of premarket jitter:

What if the place has someone else already selling? This, he decided was highly unlikely. Besides, his rhubarb flavor was surely a superior product.

What if the proper women in the community, those opposed to the Devil's liquid should catch on to him and send their men after him? Hopefully Lizzy could run if that were the case.

What if no one there wanted any, and had already adjusted to going without? Nah. Little chance of that. This place had lots of young men looking for adventure, or courage, enough at least to ask a girl to dance.

What if the constabulary were about? Nah. That too was somewhere next to nil on the chance scale. It was just too far from town.

Maybe someone would report him? Well, all he could do was his best to keep it a secret while still making sales. If someone did report him, that was another day, and by the time they came to his place, the illicit juice would be buried underground anyway, and he planned to haul the still itself even farther away, just for the winter.

He walked Lizzy a little closer, and then pulled up, tied her to a fencepost, got off, and poured back a right decent swig, to provide himself with some encouragement, out and away from his hermit shyness. He put the bag of bottles two fenceposts down from Lizzie, and commanded her, "You protect this now, Lizzy. If someone touches it, make a racket, Girl. Scare them away." Lizzy whinnied back at him, as if she understood, and off he mosied, with only his sampler bottle. He hoped he'd have some left by the time he got to the hall, and slurped back another full shot.

Because he had no intention of going into the hall, he went to where all the other horses were tied up, outside by the small stable the community had built, for real cold nights. Several buggies were sitting there, indicating that ladies were about, but mostly it appeared that people had come by horseback, as the railing held more, and he could hear a few horses grazing off about a hundred yards or so. A few families that lived within three or four miles could have hoofed it. In total, he figured about a hundred folks had gathered.

The first person he met on the cool evening was the last he'd have liked to see: Ed McMillan, his neighbour, coming out to check his buggy. No sale here. McMillan started the conversation. "Well, if it isn't my neighbour, Mr. Perkins. I didn't know you were interested in these things."

"Well, not usually. I figured I could come by once in a while, and I was getting kind of bored. There was a lot of music where I grew up, you know. Been a few years since I heard any."

Ed McMillan accepted that, and asked Swampy to join him for the walk into the hall. Swampy didn't want to go in, so he declined the invite, "I just want to hear a bit of the music, I'm not really here to dance, so I think I'll just stay outside where I can hear it."

McMillan actually preferred this. He certainly didn't want to be the fellow to bring the smelly hermit inside. The dance held classy folk, and none would be too happy, especially the women.

Soon a young couple who Swampy didn't recognize came out for a some fresh air, apparently needing it from all that dancing. Perhaps they were going for a romantic walk in the cool evening air. Swampy greeted them, "Howdy."

The young man looked at Swampy, not knowing what to make of the bearded poorly dressed critter, but introduced himself anyway, "Hi. My name is William. This is Helen. Nice night tonight, isn't it?"

"My name, son, is Sam Perkins. Yup, it sure is a nice night tonight. Damn winter is coming in, though. Hope it's not a long one, like last year."

Swampy, by now, was friendlied up a bit from the juice.

William, catching a whiff of a liquor smell amidst the other odors Swampy emitted, approached a little closer, "Is that liquor I smell on you, Mister?"

Swampy, not knowing whether the young man was upset at the smell, or inquisitive, hoping to get some, decided that he might as well go for it, "Well, yes, son, I suppose it is."

William reacted in the wrong way, "You know, Sir, that stuff is illegal. Did you have some left over after the government banned it?"

"No, Son, this is my home made stuff. It's from rhubarb," Swampy, replied, proudly.

Now more aggressive, William spoke clearly. "Well, it's illegal. My folks and I were talking about it just the other day. We figured someone the likes of you might be up to making some home made stuff, and Dad told me to watch out for it here tonight, in fact. I'm gonna go back in and tell him. If I was you, I'd probably get my butt out of here." With the threat, William, self-appointed liquor buster, turned around and stomped for the hall, to inform his Dad, Ed McMillan, and together they'd see to it that any distribution of the Devil's drink would be stopped, here and now.

Swampy spat on the ground, narrowly missing his own foot, and shrugged. He looked disheveled, and his face drooped. The expectations of huge profits from sales were about to be foiled, it seemed. The whole summer of work flashed before his eyes. All that sweat. All that hauling of wood and rhubarb. All those poor sleeps. All that pig smell around, not to mention the heroic testing on his behalf of Larry the loyal hog. He turned around and started shuffling off, back to Lizzy, who at least, was a true friend. "I guess I have plenty of stuff to drown my sorrows in," he thought. "Those ten bottles themselves should last me the winter. Too bad about the other fifty or so yet to be brewed."

But before he shuffled even ten feet, a hand grabbed his, and he turned to face Helen, who had remained outside on her own when Dan stomped righteously in. She stared him square in the eye. "Quick, Mister," she said, "tell me if you have any more."

Swampy's face lit up, as his eyes met hers. "Yup, I sure do, Miss. Follow me."

# Mother

Who knows how long the Goldeye have inhabited the Battle, but it's been off and on for awhile. A few took habitation in the creek back in the 40s or so, and again in the 70s and 80s. Unlike the jack (pike), which everyone unanimously declares as being as ugly as a rotting rat, or the walleye, of which everyone agrees as to it's natural elegance, what with perfect symmetry, fine scales, and intricately patterned fins, there are two opinions on the looks of Goldeye. The first time a fisherman lands one evokes one response, or the other.

The positive side declares: "Wow, look at that. It's so shiny and slender, yet thick from top to bottom. It's definitely unique. In the water you can see it it's shimmery whole side reflecting the light. I love it. Such a marvel of nature!"

The negative side is in contrast: "Look at the shape of *that* thing. Huge scaly critter, so flat, such beady ugly eyes, and disformed body! Yuchhh! Throw Mr. Ugly back. Reminds me of a flounder. Get it out of my sight!"

This love it or hate it stance follows through with regards to taste as well, as some guys adore the oily brown texture, while others refuse to even smell it, preferring to share it with cats.

However, there is a particular rare genetic offshoot of animals: the albino, which qualifies for a high status in the ranks of magnificent creations of nature. Perhaps it is only rarity that connotes mystique. Perhaps white symbolizes purity, cleanliness, and all things good, at least in Judaic-Christian thought. Native spiritualists, too, recognize the albino as a harbringer of change. Whatever the reasons, unquestionably, the albino maintains its mystique throughout the lore.

This albino sighting did not occur on a fishing trip, but on a berry picking campaign. Among several species of edible berries along the Battle, including saskatoon, black currants, pincherries, chokecherries, one stands out for its sheer abundance. Locally it is called the high bush cranberry, and it is only located along the Battle in extremely boggy areas close to the river where the tree roots can access tremendous loads of water, producing huge grape-like clumps, although the flat-seeded berry itself is much tinier than a grape. People familiar with it use the juice to produce a unique, offbeat tasting jelly.

Ned Perkins was along the Battle on a berry gathering expedition with his Mother, Jess. The curious ten year old was more prone to wandering, than picking.

"Neddy, we're here to pick berries, remember, not to wander all around. I want you to at least fill that pail," Mother warned him as they exited the truck.

Ned was not one to heed warnings. "I think there are better bushes over this way, Mom." Ned understood which excuses to apply, for avoiding work. Wandering off was one such excuse, as whenever there was any doubt to his motives at all, Mother would tolerate it. She didn't have a rope, after all, and she was too occupied filling her own bucket to notice, or care, exactly what he was up to.

Within five minutes, Ned was far enough that he honestly could not hear her beckoning, thanks to the thick undergrowth. He congratulated himself for escaping the torture of berrying, at least for the moment. Meandering along the flowing water of the Battle was both relaxing, and potentially far more interesting. Certainly a more intelligent choice of momentary awareness flow, unlike dull berrypicking, this was true creative laziness. He found a rock to sit upon to watch the river.

Within another five minutes, the serenity of mind was overtaken by boyhood intrinsic wanderlust, which forced him further downstream than the original plan, along a boring stretch of river. The soft gurgling of a rapid ahead catalysed deja-vu of himself sitting, as an infant, with his mother, marvelling at the gurgling. The serene vibration of the slow water nearby rubbed off, and he moved in slow motion, in contrast to the hurried rate at which he'd left the berrying task. Another hundred yards, and the wanderlust was overcome by the transcendent stillness. He sat, again, and watched. The stillness was broken by silent movement, out in the middle or the river, through the clear autumn water.

"Hmmmmmm," he thought, "a fish of some sort." He froze, instinctively, as a cat preying. Because the fish was oval shaped, and only about a foot in length, and because he'd studied his father's guide, he determined that it must be a goldeye. But this was no normal goldeye! It was different in that it was pure white, not silvery like goldeye in pictures, as if he had taken a piece of Mom's white china, and shaped it into a fish, then tossed it into the water tank. He strained for memory, for he was unsure of the existence of albino fish. This only confused his perception of reality. But soon the fish's mystical presence overcame whatever memory he carried, and he acknowledged that what he was seeing existed, regardless of what any book might say. An eternity passed, just the boy, and the marvel of nature, in the moment.

It moved along, upstream, in hesitating swishes, stopping, he supposed, to nibble on some morsel. Within time, it moved out of sight, which had little impact on him. The fact that he'd seen it at all gave him a sense of mysterious purpose, even of God.

His thoughts turned to what his mission was now. He flashed into several memories of disbelieving parents and siblings, of things he'd thought to have seen, only to be disproved, of things that he wasn't sure of, and of downright anger at being called a liar. The UFO, the skunk, the coyote close to the cattle, all the disputable events he'd had in his life flashed past his mind's eye. He felt uncomfortable, as his fist instinctively closed in response to the vivid memories.

Would this, the tale of an albino fish, become just another story to add to his file detailing hallucinations of childhood?

To tell them, his family, of this 'strange' encounter, would surely bring ridicule and disbelief. As other tales had before, it would soon spread beyond family to relatives. "Neddy says he saw an albino!" He could hear the unbearable taunts.

"I did. I did. I did." He saw himself screaming angrily, before he departed the room, to the confines of his own room, or to the confines of a walk in the bushes, alone, where he could sulk, and plot revenge on the disbelievers.

So too he pondered the choice of not telling. Perhaps he had witnessed the only albino goldeye ever. What then? Was it not his duty to inform the world? Wouldn't a biologist wish to know? Was it not their right? Wouldn't his family benefit from the exposure? If believed, or better yet if he could prove it, by catching or photographing the thing, he would no doubt become famous, at least locally. He envisioned himself in a photo, fish in hand, in the local paper, then in the city paper. The caption read: "LOCAL BOY DISCOVERS ALBINO GOLDEYE!"

He closed his eyes, to visualize it. But the fear in him changed the words to now read, "NED FINALLY COMMITTED TO INSANE ASYLUM!" The force behind this headline altered his calm, and he talked louder to the water, "Wish I hadn't seen you, you stupid fish! Look what you've done." The rock upon which he was seated induced a gentle smile when he remembered the saying, summing the situation up to himself, "Mr. Goldeye" he whispered, "You sure have me between a rock and a hard place."

His 'to tell or not to tell' dilemma only worsened as he talked angrily, then softly, to the flowing empty water. A bubble rose from beneath the rock immediately in front of him. Again he whispered, "Bubble, you must be a sign from Mr. Goldeye out there. I think you are his messenger." He watched the bubble explode as it surfaced, recognizing it as symbolic of an impending explosion in his life, should anyone else come to know of the secret he now harbored.

He looked up. A wisp of cool autumn air caught his face, and he smiled, having made the decision. "You're welcome, Mr. Goldeye." he replied, in mock conversation, believing his powerful decision could have conceivably saved the creature's life. A gentle transformation of mindset overtook him. He suddenly felt amazingly pure, energized from his lifegiving experience, and his absolute personal vow to secrecy. A decision he could look back on reflectively the rest of his life, he *knew* he would never regret it.

His adventure now complete, wanderlust satisfied, and mind set, he got up, and walked briskly away from the river, for fear that another sighting may cause him to rethink the whole darn thing. Happy now, he hurried to find a quality cranberry bush by which he could at least fill a portion of the pail, a task he had been ordered to complete, and without, he may face a few hours of criticism in his direction, from the mouth of his mother. The trail passed right past a well endowed bush, branches bent nearly to the ground, with heavy cranberry clusters. Within moments, he had the bucket three quarters full, and hurried on to be with another Mother.

"Hi, Mom," he called cheerily, when he sighted her. "I found a good bush over there. I got you a whole pail, almost full."